Convulsive

Part One

MARCUS MARTIN

ACKNOWLEDGMENTS

Parts One and Two of *Convulsive* would not have been possible without the incredible support I received from my family and friends. My sincere thanks to you all for providing me with a plethora of stylistic, scientific, and structural advice. For your patience, encouragement, and honesty, I am eternally grateful to Adrian Bonsall, Ian McNeil, John Wallis, Chris Powell, Charlie Houseago, Louise Martin, Mike Clarke, Oli Moravszky, Brian Dixon, Alex O'Bryan-Tear, Jess Donnithorne, Oliver Freeman, and Darren Coney. To Mum, Dad, Lottie, and Tania, life would be monochrome without you.

Cover art by Rob Eager:
www.facebook.com/PaperButterflyProductions

Contents

ONE

Blackout

It was almost two a.m., according to Lucy's phone. Still no signal. The sound of a key scratching its way into the lock pricked her ears.

"Luce?" came Dan's voice as the front door clicked open.

She shoved the envelope back into the drawer.

"Dan!" she cried, dashing out from the candlelit kitchen to her partner, who stood in the front doorway wearing a head lamp. "I saw your note," she quavered. "What the hell's going on?"

"I'll explain as we go. Take these," he said, panting, as he passed her two gallon-sized bottles of water. "Just leave them in the hallway. We need to be quick."

He swivelled the vast hiking backpack off his shoulders and swung it onto the floor. It was fit to burst.

"Dan, you're freaking me out. What is all this?" choked Lucy.

"Put your shoes on, there's more in the car," he panted, mopping the band of sweat from his brow and disappearing out of the door again. *"Come on!"*

Lucy hastily pulled on a pair of sneakers and set off after him, down the blacked-out stairwell.

"Dan, tell me what's going on! You leave me a note saying everything's about to change – what does that even mean?"

"Whisper," he hissed, casting his light around the deserted level. "Did you see the news? Before the networks went down?"

"I caught a bit at work – is this to do with the whole space station thing?" replied Lucy, hastening to keep up as Dan raced on.

"Yes," he said, as they rounded the corner of the sixth floor. "Dad called me right before the news broke. The White House thinks what happened to the ISS is linked to what's happening to the satellites."

"What *is* happening to them?" probed Lucy.

"I don't know, OK? All I know is what Dad told me. It's what's next that matters. *Stop!"*

He halted and covered his head lamp. Lucy froze mid-step and listened, her eyes adjusting to the darkness.

"Out, go on," crowed a smoker's voice from around the corner. "There you go. Mommy'll let you back in when it's morning."

A sliver of flickering candlelight spilled out into the stairwell, accompanied by a soft "meow", before the unseen apartment door clicked shut again and darkness returned.

Dan waited a few seconds more then uncovered his head lamp, reilluminating the stairs downward.

"Everything we use," he whispered urgently, as they continued their hurry down the levels, "phones, the internet, the national grid,

2

banks, farming, *everything* – it's all dependent on GPS; on satellites. Without GPS there's no universal time anymore. So every nation has to revert to their own alternatives, which will be fractionally different to one another. That tiny split-second difference is enough to trigger server errors across the world. Which means goodbye stock markets, goodbye currency. It also means we have to switch all our power sources back to manual, which is crazy intensive."

Dan clicked his light off again as they reached the first floor. As they approached the lobby doors he slowed to a halt. Cautiously, they stepped out onto the steep, pitch-black street. It was deserted. Vivid moonlight reflected off parked cars and curtained windows.

Dan led the way to their car and popped the trunk. It was brimming with supplies – bags of food, equipment, and water.

"Here," he said, passing her a head lamp of her own. "Don't turn it on until we're back inside."

Lucy fumbled the lamp into place.

"Did you let anyone into the apartment while I was gone?" asked Dan, heaving out six bags and handing them to Lucy.

"What? Why does that matter?" she huffed, staggering under the new weight.

"Holy shit, you did!" breathed Dan. "Was it Cassie?"

"No, she took a cab after we left the bar."

"Then who?"

"Dan, what the hell? You're acting insane. It was the lady from downstairs – from 701. She wanted a glass of water, so I gave it to her. It's not a big deal. Can we do this later? These bags are killing me."

"Jesus, Luce, I told you!" hissed Dan.

3

"Told me what, Dan?" she countered, placing the bags on the ground.

"In the note! I said be careful!"

"Oh, and from that I was supposed to get 'don't give any old ladies water because something's up with the satellites'? Yeah, *my bad*," she snapped, in a harsh whisper.

Dan bit his lip. "She'll be back tomorrow, Luce, you know that, right? For more water."

"And?"

"We don't have enough to share!" retorted Dan. "I could barely get enough for the two of us as it was. We don't know how long it's gonna be before the water comes back on, and we need enough to drink and flush out the toile—"

Dan's head snapped around. Footsteps echoed down the sidewalk. He grabbed the lip of the trunk and knelt down behind the car, pulling the trunk down silently. Lucy squinted at the dark silhouette heading in their direction. Dan tugged the hem of her jacket and she quickly crouched down beside him.

The stranger's footsteps got louder. Lucy looked at Dan; his head was bowed and turned away from the sidewalk, his eyes fixed on the ground. She copied, tilting her head downward, also covering her head with her jacket.

The figure passed by without stopping. Lucy tentatively uncovered her pale face and peered out at Dan, who was looking at her intently, a finger held up to his lips. She nodded.

The footsteps ceased a little way down the street, and they heard a door open and close. Dan indicated for Lucy to keep still while he shuffled closer to the sidewalk and leaned forwards, checking both directions, before rising to his feet and scanning the entire street.

"Clear," he whispered, opening the trunk once again.

Lucy climbed to her feet, her head rushing slightly as circulation returned to her legs. "Dan, you're scaring me now."

He hastily retrieved more bags then sealed the trunk with a quiet click. He faced her directly, five or six brimming bags in each hand. "If you're scared, it's because you're beginning to understand the situation. We need to get these inside."

They re-entered the building and switched their head lamps on, beginning the long stairwell climb. For a while they ascended in silence, the darkness punctuated only by their shallow breaths and scuffling of shoes.

"I withdrew all the money I could get from our accounts," said Dan, breaking the silence as they rounded the fifth floor. "Until the ATMs stopped working on the last one."

"You did what? You took my credit cards?" seethed Lucy. "A minute ago you were laying into *me* for giving an old lady some water!"

"*Whisper!*" insisted Dan. "Listen to me, Luce," he panted. "In six years, have I ever given you reason to doubt me?"

"No," she conceded, as they staggered upwards.

"Have I ever abused your trust, or put you in harm's way?"

"OK, Dan, I get it. But you *have* to tell me why you're doing all this."

Dan said nothing for a few steps, recovering his breath.

"Without electronic trading," he replied, finally, "our currency's going to crash. So are all the currencies, everywhere. Money means nothing now. It was the right thing to do, you have to trust me."

Lucy swallowed hard. The beam from her head lamp wobbled up a step with each foot she put forwards.

"In the morning," he puffed, "people will start to realize they have no way of accessing their banks. No way of paying for stuff. First they'll protest. Then when they realize nothing can be done, they'll panic. At the same time, some folk will have figured out that CCTV's stopped working, and alarm systems are offline."

"So … like New Orleans after Katrina."

"Exactly. Mass looting."

"And with the phones down, no one can call the cops," gasped Lucy, as they rounded another level.

"Right. Which means the looting will become more violent."

"But … in San Francisco?"

"Trust me. Take away people's power, their food and water, and there's no such thing as civilized society. Just one big tinderbox. I've seen it happen."

Lucy stopped in her tracks. "Are we gonna be safe here, Dan?"

"Keep moving," he replied, glancing back at her.

"We should get to DC. Your dad – we'd be safe with him, right?" she pressed, catching up as they reached the eighth floor.

"It's too late for that. It's a four-day drive and we'd have no way to refuel. If the government's smart, they'll declare martial law first thing tomorrow. They'll deploy the National Guard. That'll restore order."

"Are you gonna get called up?" said Lucy, aghast, as they reached their apartment.

"No, luckily my rank was too junior for that," replied Dan, lowering half of his bags and taking out the key.

Lucy's arms burned as he opened their front door. Dan grabbed the lowered bags and staggered inside to the end of their hallway, where he abandoned both handfuls and sat down on the ground. Lucy kicked the door closed with her foot and ditched her bags immediately, sliding down onto the floor adjacent to Dan.

"We're safe here," he panted. "So long as no one knows we've got a stockpile. Do you understand? That's why water lady can't come here again."

"Her name's Manuela," said Lucy, mopping her brow. The beam from her head lamp crossed Dan's midway along the corridor floor. She clicked off the flashlight.

"In the next seven days, Luce, things are going to change beyond recognition. In this city it's you and me now, no one else. It has to be."

She nodded but said nothing. Her mind slid from their Spanish neighbour in 701, whom she would no longer assist, to her best friend, whom she'd spent the evening with only a few hours prior. The latter was harder to abandon. She couldn't just cut the rope.

"Come on," said Dan, standing up and holding out a hand for Lucy. "We need to get the rest from the car. Two more trips."

Lucy took his hand and clicked her light back on. She knew she could trust Dan with her life. And she knew he was right. But she had to warn Cassie.

TWO

Fault Lines

The mid-morning sun shone like it was any other day. But at street level, a different story was unfolding. Lucy kept her foot hovering over the brake pedal and edged forwards using the clutch. Horns blared all around as drivers tried to negotiate intersections without working signals.

As they left the freeway, it became apparent that San Jose was behaving much the same as San Francisco had been. The streets were teeming with people walking around holding their phones up, trying to find a signal. A café was giving away its melting stocks of ice cream and other dairy products. Handwritten *CASH ONLY* signs were taped to the windows of the handful of open stores they'd passed so far.

"Here!" said Dan, pointing to a turning to the strip mall. "It's second from the end."

The stores were all unusually dark, and the parking lots were empty by Saturday's standards. Lucy parked up outside the modest-sized gun store.

"You sure he'll remember you?" she asked, climbing out of the driver's seat and stretching in the adjacent empty parking space, taking in the store's sloping red tiles and salmon-coloured art-deco crown.

"Are you for real? We toured together," replied Dan, with a slight puff of his chest.

"Yeah, but you haven't seen him in, what, three years?" said Lucy, locking their ageing Ford Focus and following after him.

"He'll remember me," said Dan, approaching the store entrance. "He owes me a favour."

Red Wood Tactical read the swirling crimson signage on the white store banner. The lights were off but the steel shutters were raised, revealing the window displays of encased rifles and accessories. The glass front door was propped open by a trashcan.

"Hello?" Dan called out, stepping inside with Lucy in tow.

"Can I help you?" came a hostile voice from the gloomy counter.

"Morning, sir," replied Dan, warmly. "I'm looking for AJ, is he around?"

"Do I look like AJ?" retorted the middle-aged proprietor. "No. I do not. Therefore y'all may reasonably deduce that 'AJ' *ain't* around."

"And I could reasonably deduce that you're a grade 'A' asshole," chipped in Lucy. "Come on, Dan, this is clearly the wrong place. Screw this guy."

"I'm merely stating the facts, miss," replied the man, his tinted brown glasses standing out against his wrinkled white skin.

"I think I know exactly what you're stating," railed Lucy.

"Luce, it's fine," soothed Dan, who addressed the proprietor once again. "Do you know where AJ's store is, sir?"

"AJ don't *have* a store anymore. Y'all can't've been that close if y'all didn't hear. Your boy went cuckoo. State withdrew his licence to sell firearms. As they tend to do with crazy people. So he sold up."

"To you?" said Dan.

"Smart fella, ain't ya," replied the man, setting his elbows on the counter and leaning on them with a grin.

"We need to buy two handguns," said Lucy, cutting across Dan's faltering smile.

"Pick any one you like," replied the owner, gesturing generously.

"We also need to take them home today," she added.

"Now that," replied the man, straightening up again, "is called *i-l-l-e-g-a-l*. Y'all are clearly feds. I don't see a warrant, so how's about y'all just piss off my property right now."

"We're not feds," Dan assured him. "I used to serve with AJ, which is why we came here. We need to buy a couple of guns, but we were kinda hoping we could … *speed along* the whole ten-day background check thing. We can pay you well for it."

"Uh-huh," replied the man. "If you wanna speed things up, why don't you take those nigger legs of yours and run along then?"

Lucy's jaw dropped. "You – you *deplorable* –"

Dan took her by the arm and steered her out of the store before she could fully articulate the extent of her rage.

"What a … a …" Lucy stuttered.

"He was a real charmer," sighed Dan, stepping around to the passenger side of the car.

"But, you shouldn't have to –"

"Luce, it's fine," he smiled, kindly. "Old white guy running a gun shop? The odds were always stacked against him."

She fished the keys from her bag. "Are you OK?"

"I'm concerned. If Colonel Sanders in there is anything to go by, it looks like no one's gonna skip the background checks for the sake of a couple of strangers. He wasn't interested in being bribed, which kinda limits our options."

"And AJ was your only contact?"

"There's one other place we could try," said Dan, scratching his chin. "But it's more of a long shot. I'd be playing the veteran card. It's an army surplus store back in the city. They *might* help us out."

"We're gonna have to hurry," said Lucy. "You saw the people outside the banks earlier. They're starting to figure out what's going on."

***

The freeway spat them back out in San Francisco a good hour later, where they began to crawl once more through the gridlocked inner-city traffic. It had worsened in the few hours they'd been gone.

"Try changing to long wave," said Lucy from the driving seat, as Dan scrolled through the FM radio stations to no avail. He duly switched and a station crackled into life: KGO 810 was still on air, despite the power cut.

"… are asking, 'Is this a government takeover, and should we be resisting it?'" said the presenter, as Dan tuned in.

"That sounds positive," quipped Lucy.

"The headlines again," continued the newsreader. "The president has declared a national state of emergency following the loss of global satellite communications. This comes less than twenty-four hours after the government forced the stock exchanges to close early. There's been widespread failure of cell networks, as well as the loss of internet access and electronic banking services.

"The president has mandated that food and water rations be distributed countrywide within the next seven days – a sign that the White House is anticipating ongoing disruption. This followed the announcement that the National Guard are being deployed across every city in the country. Which brings us back to this morning's hot topic: conspiracy or calamity? Our first guest in the studio is Dr Adriana St–"

Dan flicked the radio off.

"I'm not sure I can handle their 'experts' right now," he said, as Lucy nudged the car forwards.

The roads made for infuriatingly slow progress, as every junction had to be approached with extreme caution now that the lights were out. Not that everyone was cautious. Lucy edged past another crammed bus bearing the brunt of the cancelled tram service.

"I think it's left here," said Dan, as they crawled towards another locked-up intersection.

Lucy hit the indicator, which clicked away busily in their motionless car. "We're not gonna make it in time, Dan. They'll know what's going on by the time we get there. Other people will be listening to those radio reports."

"We have to try," he replied, while peering out of the window.

A stressed-looking traffic cop stopped them at the interchange, waving through a row of traffic from the adjacent side, before stopping that flow of traffic and rotating to a new lane. It took about four minutes before the cop returned to Dan and Lucy's lane and signalled it was their turn to move off.

With one hand pointed at them, his other hand signalled the oncoming lane to stop. But three advancing cars began to accelerate. The cop's whistle slipped a little as his jaw slackened, and his eyes widened in disbelief. He began furiously blowing and gesturing at them to stop, but it had no effect; the young drivers tore past him, flipping him the bird as they went. He grabbed his radio and barked flustered descriptions of the cars into it, then let it fall limply back into place on his drooped shoulder, as his eyes followed the last vehicle swerving off into the distance.

Some people behind began to lean on their horns and the cop snapped back to reality, hastily waving Lucy and Dan through.

"Go left here," instructed Dan, directing her onto a quieter backstreet. "We might be able to circumvent some of this traffic."

Up ahead two men were hammering a large piece of wooden panelling to a convenience-store window, a pile of smashed glass beneath their boots.

"Are you sure, Dan? I'm not feeling this neighbourhood so much."

A rusty white car pulled up alongside a decrepit blue Cadillac in front of them. A hand extended out of the white car's window and was met by another from the Cadillac. The exchange only took an instant, then the rusty white car was gone.

Lucy determinedly avoided making eye contact with the parked-up dealers and picked up the pace to get past them.

Further down the street a woman was walking down the sidewalk clad in a large sandwich board with the word *REPENT* printed across it. Odd snippets of the woman's doomsday proclamations made it through into the car as they drove past, her words interspersed with the colourful array of insults being hurled at her by a pack of teenagers loitering on a corner not far from where she marched. The teens were falling about with laughter, doing impressions of the lady, making crude sexual gestures at her, while she for her part instructed them in vivid detail about how exactly they were all going to burn in the fires of hell for eternity. The teens didn't seem overly concerned by that.

"Hey, Luce, pull over! Pull over – right there, a payphone! Why didn't I think of it before?"

"Pull over? Here? Do you want us to get mugged?"

"We'll be quick – but this could be our only chance! I need to try and speak to Dad again, he said something was … I just need to speak to him, alright?"

Lucy looked around in the mirrors; the blue Cadillac was out of sight now, and the teens were a good way off.

"OK," she said, bringing the car up to the sidewalk, "but I don't see what good it'll do if the networks are down."

"Payphones get their power direct from the landline phone network," said Dan, pushing the door open. "They're separate to the rest of the grid!"

Lucy got out with him. Cigarette butts dotted the pavement, the nicotine ghosts of recent callers. By the looks of it, those people – wherever they were now – had been standing in line for some time.

The phone hung freely off its hook about a yard from the dirty concrete ground, swinging fractionally in a micro convection current.

Dan picked the receiver up and put it to his ear, shoving a handful of quarters into the coin slot.

"Come on ... come *on* ..." he muttered as he punched in the number. "*Please* ..." After a long pause he slumped forwards, pressing his head against the wall in disappointment.

"No luck?" asked Lucy, placing a consoling hand on his shoulder.

"I think the landline network's down too. So much for my theory," he replied, slamming the receiver back into its holster.

Lucy looked at the stickers of the local hookers that lined the walls of the booth.

"Let's get back in the car," she said, leading the way.

As she climbed back into the driving seat, metallic rattles echoed down the street. Lucy watched through the rear-view mirror as the youths threw empty beer cans at the doomsday lady. Apparently her attempts to baptize them were less than welcome.

"We should keep looking for phone booths as we go," said Dan. "Maybe that one was a blip. Stop if you see one, yeah?"

"How about we just focus on getting the gun first," said Lucy, pulling away with a wary eye on the teenagers.

"We can do both," insisted Dan. "The surplus store can't be far from here. We're in the right area. We need to head right – here."

Lucy slowed to a crawl as they had done for most of the junctions to date and caught a snapshot of conversation from the locals loitering outside their homes. Wherever they'd driven that day, the talk had been the same. *None of my shit's working ... I can't get on Facebook ... How am I supposed to watch my show now?* Lucy was shocked at how myopic the complaints were. It was like no one else was taking the situation seriously. Maybe some of them were – but they weren't the ones people-watching and drinking beer from their porches.

As she swung the car right, they were met by a police roadblock stretching across both sides of the street. A lone cop stood before them, his car turned side-on to the traffic flow, its lights flashing and a small orange wing of cones extending from either side, along with tyre-shredding spike strips.

"You'll have to turn around here folks, this road's closed," said the officer, one hand conspicuously resting on his gun holster.

"OK, officer. Can I ask why the road's closed?" Lucy replied.

"There's a minor disturbance up ahead. We're just taking precautionary measures to keep the situation under control."

"A disturbance?" questioned Lucy. "We're trying to get to the army surplus store. Will we be able to take a different route there?"

"I wouldn't head there, ma'am, that's where the trouble is. Believe me, you don't wanna get caught up in that. Best head home, if I were you. Most of the stores are closed now anyhow."

"We just –" began Dan, but Lucy interrupted, seeing the officer's hand move to his holster and slowly pop the button.

"Of course, officer. Thank you for your help," she said, putting the car into reverse and carefully turning it around.

"What did you cut me off for?" protested Dan as they left the cop.

"He was reaching for his gun, Dan! That guy was jumpy. I didn't wanna piss him off. He's probably more on edge than we are – think about it, those guys are on the front line for whatever happens now."

She looked into the rear-view mirror where the cop was talking into his radio as he rushed back to his car.

"Look!" she exclaimed, pointing to the mirror.

Dan turned in his seat, craning his neck to see behind him.

The officer slammed the door shut as he hurled himself into the driver's seat and sped off down the street he'd closed, abandoning the traffic cones and spike strips behind him. Clearly the "minor disturbance" he'd referred to was becoming less minor.

"So your surplus place is out, then," said Lucy, turning to Dan. "What now?"

"I don't know," sighed Dan, rubbing his face.

"Might be time to cut our losses," suggested Lucy, tentatively.

"Agreed," conceded Dan. "But keep looking for payphones on the way back. You never know."

They continued to weave through the backstreets, avoiding the snared-up traffic arteries.

"Wait up," said Dan, several minutes later, pointing across the road. "We should stop there."

Lucy followed his line of sight to the drug store up ahead. As she pulled off the main road into the parking lot, a man hurried out and away from the store with something tucked firmly under his arm. He repeatedly checked over his shoulder as he rushed back to his car and away from the store.

Alongside the grocery displays, the windows were covered by pharmaceutical stickers and posters designed to convince you that your life would implode unless you took their latest drug.

"Have you got the money?" said Lucy, quietly, as they exited the car.

"Yup. Let's be quick, though," replied Dan, as he followed Lucy to the entrance.

17

She pushed one of the heavy, formerly automatic doors open and stepped inside the darkened store. Immediately before them stood a broad, suited man around seven feet tall, and a good three feet wide. His head was shaven, but his face was decorated by a long scar running from above one eye down to his cheekbone. Nestled next to the vertical line was the pockmark scarring of severe acne, giving the man something of a textured look. An ill-fitting black goatee jutted downwards from his chin, pointing towards a creased tie and a thick leather belt. His massive hands were clasped neatly over the buckle. Lucy's eyes clocked the gold knuckleduster on his right hand, and as they approached he made a point of flashing his jacket back to show a couple of concealed handguns strapped to his body.

"Security," he said bluntly as he blocked Lucy's path. "Him first," he said, gesturing to Dan to spread his arms in a T-shape.

"Are you serious?" said Dan, lifting his arms as the giant, who reeked of BBQ sauce, began patting him down for weapons.

Once satisfied Dan was clean, the man moved on to Lucy. She couldn't tell if it was fear warping her perception, or if he really did spend longer on her than Dan, but it felt like a small eternity as his rough hands moved over her body. Finally, he stepped aside, waving them through with a slight cock of the head and a grunt.

They entered the drugstore. It was gloomy, the sunlight outside struggling to penetrate the layer of neurosis-inducing film that covered the store windows. Lucy blinked, trying to adjust her eyes to the new surroundings. At the back of the store, behind a counter cordoning off the prescription drugs, stood a stern-looking woman. Her face was cold, severe, and calculating. As they approached the desk, Lucy was acutely aware that drugstores did not usually have security with knuckledusters. She was already starting to regret their decision.

"Hey there," began Dan.

The woman didn't so much as blink.

"Excuse me," he persisted. "We need some antibiotics please."

"Amoxicillin," whispered Lucy, leaning into Dan's ear. "My doctor gave it to me when I had strep throat. I remember her saying it was broad spectrum."

Dan turned back to the woman behind the counter. "How much for a course of amoxicillin?"

"Four hundred dollars," replied the woman.

"How much?" blurted Lucy.

"Bitch, you deaf?" snapped the lady. "Four hundred. Per pack."

Lucy looked around at Dan incredulously, then back at the woman's dispassionate face. "Are you serious? Those pills have been off patent for decades. They're generic, they cost like half a cent to produce!"

"And now they cost four hundred dollars to buy."

"That's extortion!" cried Lucy.

"Omar!" yelled the woman, calling the giant security guard over.

"OK, OK, no need for that," said Dan, drawing out his bulging wallet. "We'll take them."

"What?" objected Lucy, but Dan ignored her.

"And we'll take some fluco ... fluco ... dammit, what's it called?"

"Flucloxacillin!" snapped Lucy, still seething.

"Yes! We'll take some of that too."

"That stuff's five hundred," said the woman.

"Will you do me three packs of each for two thousand?" asked Dan, counting out two thousand dollars.

"Jesus, Dan, what are you doing?" hissed Lucy, trying to wrestle his outstretched hands away from the counter while the woman stared at him, boring into his soul with her mercenary eyes. He finished counting and held out the wad.

The lady looked them both up and down several times.

"Deal," she finally uttered, immediately snatching the money from Dan's hand. She held the notes up over her shoulder, and called out behind her without taking her eyes off Dan. "Kyle!"

A thin, nervous-looking younger man emerged from the back of the pharmacy section. From the age gap, he could have been her son, or her lover, Lucy couldn't tell which. Either way, the relationship looked deeply unhealthy.

"Four packs of pills for the white girl," snapped the woman.

"We said six packs!" protested Dan.

"Yeah? And now I say it's four packs. Or you wanna piss me off some more and make it two?"

Dan bit his lip and said nothing, but Lucy heard one of his knuckles crack as his fists clenched by his side. Omar heard the crack too and rustled behind them as he shifted weight from one giant foot to the other, readying himself for the fight.

"What ... what medication did you want?" said the nervous pharmacy assistant, looking at Lucy and Dan.

"Amoxicillin and flucloxacillin," said Dan, through clenched teeth.

"Exactly! That's what I *said*, ain't it?" cried the woman, slamming the counter with her hand. "Now go *get it*."

Dan and Lucy stood rooted to the spot. No one spoke as they waited. The woman's cold eyes fixed on Lucy, who clenched her core as tightly as she could to suppress the tremor creeping into her stance.

After a few minutes, the boy returned carrying four packets of antibiotics, which he placed down on the counter.

"That box says ampicillin," Lucy whispered to Dan.

"What's that, white girl? These ain't good enough for you?" jeered the woman.

Lucy's eyes fell on a thin trail of blood droplets that led from the counter off into the back of the pharmacy.

"No, these are fine," replied Lucy, reaching out to pick up the packs.

"Ah-ah," said the woman, casting her hand out and grabbing Lucy's before it touched any of the packets.

Her powerful fingers squeezed hard around Lucy's wrist; long, sharp nail extensions dug into Lucy's skin.

"Let me get you a bag for that," sneered the woman, smiling for the first time as she reached under the counter and retrieved a branded bag into which she began ceremoniously placing each pack. Lucy preferred the woman's previous expression to the unsettled smile now residing on her lips. "Have a great day," crowed the woman, as she placed the last pack into the bag and slid the lot over the counter. Dan grabbed the package without another word and took Lucy by the hand, hastening from the shop, squeezing past Omar who made no effort to get out of their way.

They pulled the car doors open and threw themselves inside the vehicle. Lucy tried to put the keys in the ignition, but her hands were shaking violently. Dan reached over and helped steady her, his own hands cold and clammy.

"Let's go," he said, a thought that hardly needed to be articulated, with Omar's gaze once again upon them from his new sentry post outside the store front.

Lucy revved the engine and pulled out of the parking lot at speed, only to immediately swerve out of the way as two black SUVs came screaming around the corner and across her lane.

"Jesus Christ!" Dan shouted, looking over his shoulder. Lucy instinctively flinched at the ensuing racket, staring into the mirror as bullets sprayed from the SUVs' windows, cutting Omar down where he stood. Half a dozen men with semi-automatics and handguns leapt from the vehicles and stormed the drugstore, with more gunshots ensuing as Lucy drove as fast as she could in the opposite direction.

"What the fuck just happened? What the *fuck* just happened?" she screamed, as they hurtled down the long road.

"Just keep driving, Luce, don't think about it, OK?" said Dan, his own voice wavering. His tongue tripped over syllables as he spoke. "It's gone. *They've* gone … It's happened. We need to get home. We can think about it there." His neck was craned backwards, looking for signs of pursuit. "We can think there," he said again, as he turned to face forward, the colour drained from his cheeks.

"Home?" replied Lucy, equally pale. "The city's going to shit and it's day one! This is San Francisco, for Christ's sake, and they just executed someone in broad daylight! Jesus, Dan, we have to get out of here completely!"

"And go where, Luce? Where do we go? You know what Dad said – everywhere will be turning like this now. *Everywhere.* We've gotta get home and lay low. We've got everything we need now. We just need to get home."

"Oh my god, Cassie!" cried Lucy. "She doesn't have any idea what's going on – Dan, we have to warn her!"

"What? Are you for real?"

"She's vulnerable, Dan! Look what just nearly happened to us – and that's us trying to prepare. What chance is she gonna stand on her own? We *need* to tell her what's happening!"

Dan shook his head, over and over. "No way. You're in shock. We need to get back to the apartment and calm down."

"Calm down? After that? We need to find a freakin' nuclear bunker, Dan, that's what we need!"

"We can't just … Luce, just … just focus on driving. We need to pay attention. I think we're lost."

Lucy wiped her cheeks with her sleeve and tightened her grip on the wheel as she raced down the empty side street.

"Dan," she said, suddenly decelerating as they coursed towards a static intersection with the main road. "This isn't a negotiation. We're going to Cassie, and we're going to warn her about what's ahead."

Dan patted his thighs with exasperation. "She's a grown woman, Lucy. She'll figure it out, and she'll be fine."

"She'll be 'fine'?" said Lucy. "Like we were nearly 'fine' back there? Two more minutes in that drugstore, Dan, and that would've been us!"

"Which is exactly why we can't be taking other people under our wing right now. We've gotta sort ourselves out first," said Dan, flipping the sun visor away with frustration.

"'Other people'? She's not 'other people', Dan, she's my best friend! Listen to yourself! She's your friend too!"

"And I'm saying, much as I like Cassie, we're on the brink of a global catastrophe, and to be perfectly frank, Lucy, I can't be her babysitter. She needs to look after herself."

"What would you do if I said that about Kim? Hey? If your sister lived here, in San Francisco, right now, and I turned around and said, 'To hell with her, we can't babysit other people'? I'm pretty sure you'd end our relationship on the spot."

"That's *completely* different!" retorted Dan. "For one, Cassie's not your sister, she's your friend – one of many!"

"Oh *bull*," snapped Lucy. "Don't play that card, Dan. I'm not as lucky as you, OK? I wasn't born with a sister. But I have a best friend who is *like* a sister to me, and as my partner that should be damned well good enough for you!"

Lucy swore and thumped the horn as a fleeting gap in the traffic ahead immediately resealed itself.

Dan spoke again. "As your partner, Lucy, my duty is to look after you. Not your nightmare of a friend."

"My what?" Lucy's voice shifted sharply downwards as she again tightened her grip on the steering wheel.

"You know what I'm saying, Lucy. I'm saying the truth: Cassie's a liability. Alright? I know it, you know it, anybody who meets her knows it. You really want to bring that sort of chaos into our survival chances?"

"Fucking *stop it* already!" cried Lucy, crunching on the handbrake with a jolt and turning to Dan. The film of tears covering her eyes reduced his face to a blur until she blinked them into clarity.

"I get it, OK?" she said, struggling to control the quiver in her voice. "I get that you're going into military mode to keep us safe, and keep us alive, but I can't suddenly pretend like we're the only two people in this city. Cassie has no one, OK? You've got my back, I've got yours. Who's got hers? Exactly."

"So that's my fault now, is it? That Cassie screwed things up with Myles," said Dan, throwing his hands up despairingly.

Lucy laughed in disbelief. "Don't even go there, Dan."

"Lucy, where do we draw the line? Our obligation to other people? I care about Cassie too –"

Lucy snorted.

"But if we check on her today," Dan went on, "are we gonna check on her tomorrow as well? If she runs out of food, are we gonna feed her? Are we gonna let her stay at our place if she gets scared?"

"Maybe all of that! Yeah!" said Lucy. "Why the hell not?"

"OK, great. Then who else are we gonna look after? Who are we gonna feed? Manuela? Some other neighbours? A few homeless people we stumble across? Orphaned children? Everyone deserves to eat, right? So why don't we feed them all?" said Dan, gesturing broadly in mock generosity. "We *can't*, Lucy!" he continued, slapping his hands down onto his thighs. "We *can't*. It's that simple. This situation is like nothing we've ever faced, ever – and I don't just mean you and me, I mean as a *species*. It's going to divide us into two groups: people who can make competent decisions, and people who don't. If we let ourselves get dragged down by people who don't give a shit and just live life on a whim, then we're only reducing our own chances of surviving this crisis. If we keep sharing, our resources will get used up quicker than we could ever replenish them, and we'll end up starving to death along with our dependents."

"So just to be clear," replied Lucy, "you're basically confirming that we're gonna die? Thanks, Dan. You really are the best in a crisis."

"Are you insane?" he spat, the temple in his forehead bulging. "How *dare* you! Because of me, we have a head start. We have a fighting chance, and you're throwing that back in my face? Maybe I should just pack it all in. Hell, I'll be more like Cassie, add nothing and drain everyone else's resources!"

Lucy didn't acknowledge him. Instead, she wiped her face dry and released the handbrake, forcing their car forwards into the traffic with pre-emptively aggressive beeping.

Twenty minutes passed and neither of them spoke. Now that they were back on the main streets, they'd advanced no more than a mile in the gridlocked traffic. Eventually, Dan broke the silence.

"I'm sorry," he said, staring straight ahead.

Lucy said nothing. Dan took a deep breath and tried again.

"You're right," he confessed. "If you'd said that to me about Kim, I'd have flipped out. I know Cassie's like a sister to you, and as your partner, that should have been good enough for me." He took another deep breath. "So from now on, we'll look out for Cassie as we'd look out for any other member of each other's family."

"Oh yeah," bristled Lucy. "My massive, burdensome family. Tell me, Dan, are you glad I don't come with strings attached? Does it make this whole situation easier for you?"

"I didn't mean it like that," he back-pedalled. "I meant … Cassie's family to you, so she's family to me too. OK? Jeez, I'm trying to fix things here. You could at least meet me halfway."

The tick-tock of the indicator filled another long silence as Lucy slowly took them across a chaotic intersection.

"OK," she said, after some time.

"We can head there now, if you like," offered Dan, taking more steadying deep breaths.

"Thank you," said Lucy, still not looking at him.

Lucy took in the street ahead. It was a far cry from the bloodshed they'd narrowly escaped. An enterprising bar had set up a cash-only pop-up stall outside its powerless premises and was doing roaring trade with passers-by. They even had a battery-powered boom box pumping out the latest hits. The clientele were enjoying animated conversations with each other about the peculiar goings-on of the day.

"That was pretty much all our money back there, anyway," said Dan, looking out of the side window as they drove. "If we want things now, we're gonna have to get creative about acquiring them."

**

"Man, she did well to get this place. Talk about timing," said Dan, as, a good hour later, they climbed the three steps up to Cassie's front door.

"Maybe we'll get a place by the water someday," said Lucy, knocking loudly. "You know, once the whole global satellite crisis has blown over."

She flipped Dan a hint of a smile.

"Hey, word on the street is that money's cheap these days," replied Dan, flicking up the collar of his jacket and pretending to slick back his hair. "Perfect time to put an offer on a few beach properties. If you want, I could talk to some people, who know some people, who might just know what time it is." He leaned flirtatiously against the door.

Lucy knocked again several times.

"Come on, sleazy real-estate guy," she said, giving Dan a light shove and leading the way. "Let's go around the back."

"Reliving the glory days, are we?" said Dan, feigning a swagger.

"Hey, knock it off. I'm still at least twenty per cent mad at you. Let's just try and see if she's in, OK?"

They made their way around to Cassie's modest back garden. Lucy pressed her face against the glass sliding door and tapped.

"What can you see?" asked Dan, hanging back.

"Not a lot," replied Lucy. "It's pretty dark in there. No candles or anything, so I'm guessing she's out."

"You wanna leave her a note?" suggested Dan, pulling a pen out of his pocket. "I don't have any paper – there might be a magazine in the car that we could use?"

"I've got a napkin – thanks," said Lucy, accepting Dan's pen and retrieving the unused napkin from her pocket.

Call me, Lucy began to write, immediately realizing how stupid that was. She crossed it out and started over. *Cass, we came to check you're OK. Dan's Dad says things are going to get worse – come to us if you need anything. Lucy x*

She just about managed to fit the message into the available space, then folded it in half. She quickly reopened it and added the date, before temporarily storing the note in her pocket.

"What the hell is that stuff?" called Dan from the far end of the garden, facing out across the bay. Lucy walked over and joined him, looking down at the shoreline below.

A layer of mustard-yellow liquid extended all the way across the beach as far as Lucy could see. Each crashing wave pasted a fresh coat of the substance onto the beach. It clung to the sand even as the foaming waters retreated between surges.

"It looks like oil … apart from the colour," remarked Lucy, looking further out to sea for signs of a slick. "Ever seen anything like this before?"

"I'm guessing it's a chemical spill of sorts," replied Dan. "Either way, chemical or oil, it can't be good news "

"Hey, you see that?" piped Lucy, pointing further along the beach at a white tent. The area surrounding the tent was cordoned off, save for a large white van which was parked inside the police boundary. "What do you make of it?"

"No idea. Wanna take a closer look?" asked Dan, squinting down at the tent.

"Not really," said Lucy, "and I definitely don't wanna get too close to that water. But …"

"But you think whatever's in the tent could be linked to the yellow water?" said Dan, heavily.

"Yeah. And if it's a sign of what's to come, we might as well stay ahead and find out now."

"Come on," said Dan. "Let's do it."

Lucy led the way down to the beach, clocking the police car parked at the edge of the road where the cordon began. It took them five minutes of brisk walking to reach the tent.

"It's a female officer," said Lucy, as they got closer. "You have to distract her while I check out the tent."

"What?" objected Dan. "Why can't we just ask?"

"Why do you think? Quit whining, you'll be great."

"Lucy," protested Dan. "If history taught us one thing, it's that flirting's not my strong suit. I honestly think you'd have a better chance."

"You'll be great, you're a natural," dismissed Lucy, as the officer stepped out of her vehicle to block the path.

"This route's off-limits, folks," stated the policewoman, unfathomable behind her black sunglasses, hand pre-emptively resting on her holster.

"I like your hat," said Dan, with a pathetic whimper.

"Is that a joke?" replied the officer sternly, raising an eyebrow.

"Oh, for fuck's sake, Dan," said Lucy, brushing him aside. "I apologize for my partner, officer. We were hoping you might be able to tell us what's in the tent."

"All I know is that it's off-limits to the public," shrugged the officer, her speech ever so slightly impeded by the chewing gum rotating in her mouth. "I only took over this shift an hour ago, and it's been sealed up that whole time."

"Oh, OK," said Lucy, politely. "Do you know if it's got anything to do with that weird yellow stuff on the water?" she said, gesturing to the beach.

"Look, miss, I know about as much as you know. If you wanna know more, I suggest you go down to City Hall and ask one of them."

As the officer spoke, one of the side flaps of the tent opened and a worker in a white hazmat suit exited, walking over to the van and retrieving something from the back. In that fleeting moment, Lucy glimpsed something resembling a small whale carcass inside the tent, which appeared to be covered in the sticky yellow liquid.

"Aw shit," said the cop, following Lucy's gaze over to the tent as the worker left the van with a large saw and re-entered the tent, again momentarily exposing the carcass inside.

"You folks need to leave *now*," said the officer, grinding her teeth down on the chewing gum.

"Understood," said Dan, backing away with both hands raised.

"Apologies for the inconvenience, officer," said Lucy, optimistically casting her eyes over the sealed tent once again. Defeated, she withdrew with Dan.

"Did you see that?" said Lucy as they hurried back to the car.

"I saw something. Looked like a dead whale," replied Dan, still casting his eyes back at the cop, who had returned to her car and was conveying something on the radio.

"Yeah, a dead whale covered in that yellow stuff," said Lucy, surveying the beachfront. "It's gotta be toxic, whatever it is."

"Maybe. Sometimes dead whales do just wash up, though," countered Dan. "They could be unrelated."

"But we don't usually put dead whales in freaky CSI tents under police guard," said Lucy as they neared the car. "Gimme two secs," she added, darting back to Cassie's front door quickly. She knocked a few more times, then left the note in Cassie's mailbox.

Lucy's mind played the two tent glimpses on a loop as they rejoined the city traffic. She drummed her fingers across the leather steering wheel. Fragments of her first-year dissection classes at veterinary college wove into the daydreaming. She wanted to know what species that whale had been, and what had killed it.

"Personally, I'm good," interrupted Dan.

"Huh?" replied Lucy, jolting back to the present.

"You're thinking about the tent. I can see it on your face," he continued. "Big dead whale being cut to pieces, poisonous yellow liquid? That's enough detail for me now, thanks."

"I forget how squeamish you are – for an ex-army tough guy," teased Lucy.

"Yup, that's me. Nothing says tough guy quite like majoring in philosophy," grinned Dan.

"I remember one time in a high-school biology class, we had to dissect a pig heart," said Lucy, smiling, "and all the popular girls were grossed out. Some of them literally wouldn't touch it. Some of the guys too. Of course, to me, *that* was weird, because ... well, why wouldn't you? It's just nature, right?"

"On behalf of squeamish ex-army tough guys across the world, I'm gonna go ahead and say that feeling something's heart in your hand is a slightly unsettling experience."

Lucy shrugged. "It's no different to eating meat. Granted, it doesn't smell as good as a seasoned steak."

"I think growing up on a farm may have hardened you slightly, Luce – to the vulgarities of nature."

"I wouldn't call it 'vulgar'. It just … is what it is," she mused. "But you're right about the hardening bit – ranching isn't for the faint-hearted."

The traffic slowed to a stop.

"What's that noise?" said Dan, sitting upright.

Lucy wound down the window. The shouts and cries of a panicking crowd grew closer. The people in the cars ahead began climbing out to get a better view.

"I'm gonna take a look," said Dan, opening his door.

Gunshots rang out into the air, followed by more screams. The people up ahead ducked, crawling back into their vehicles.

"Get down!" yelled Dan, crouching behind the passenger door and scrambling into the footwell.

Lucy frantically unclipped her safety belt and slid down into her own footwell. The car squealed as she accidentally nudged the accelerator with her knee, making the handbrake groan.

"What's happening?" she whispered.

He clenched his fist and raised it slightly, at a right angle to his upper arm, in the military 'stop' pose, and stared at her intensely. She didn't move a muscle.

Several minutes passed. They crouched in silence. The screams and shouts outside became more sporadic, more isolated. Two more gunshots rang out, followed by the sound of a car screeching away. Dan held his fist up again. Neither of them moved.

Another engine started, much closer this time. The whole car shook as the vehicle in front reversed directly into them, jolting Lucy and Dan's heads against the dashboard, and slamming Dan's door back shut.

The car ahead did a screeching turn on the spot and disappeared away from the commotion. Lucy looked to Dan, who raised himself up from the footwell with extreme caution, while signalling to her to stay hidden.

He peered out through the windscreen as a hacking chorus of engines restarting filled the air.

"I think it's over," whispered Dan, still scanning the foreground, poised like a hare. "Are you hurt?"

"No," said Lucy, swallowing hard. Her legs felt weak. Her head was growing dizzy.

"Sit up slowly," coached Dan, still scanning their surroundings. "Take three slow deep breaths, then come round to my side. I'll drive us back."

***

The detour Dan found for them spared Lucy whatever it was he'd seen unfold. They briefly tuned back into KGO 810 and garnered what new information there was, until the station returned to a padding loop of speculation again. When they arrived back home Dan lit a candle in the living room, and they lay entwined on the sofa for a while not talking. Lucy allowed herself to be mesmerized by the silence and warmth of the candlelight.

"Thank you – for earlier," she said, later that evening, after they'd both forced some cold food down.

"No thanks needed. I'm just glad we got out OK," he replied, glancing up from the ration count he was undertaking.

"What happened?" asked Lucy, drawing the blanket in closer around her as she perched on the bar stool.

"Some guys robbed a local bank. They didn't use detonators or anything, so I'm guessing they weren't professionals. But they had automatic weapons, so they weren't angels either. Just opportunists. I think they figured out the cameras weren't working so took their chance. Simple as that."

"What about the shooting? Was anyone hurt?"

Dan leaned in to examine an item on his list.

"Dan?" persisted Lucy.

"Yes," he answered, not looking up.

"Oh," said Lucy, quietly, blushing, her eyes falling on the floor.

Dan continued rummaging and scribbling for a few more minutes, then stood up straight.

"Done," he declared, tossing the biro onto the table. "We're good for four weeks. I've laid everything out in groups, so we can keep track of what we're using. I think we should leave it on the side. It's good to see how much food we've got left – we don't ever wanna risk getting caught out."

"OK," said Lucy, with a nod. She shivered as a cocktail of gratitude, fear, and guilt washed over her. Unlike the rest of the population, they were ready.

THREE

Cassie

---

30 HOURS EARLIER. MIDDAY, FRIDAY.

"Hey Myles," said Lucy, cornering her boss as he stood by the water cooler wearing another awful black turtleneck, "about that design for the Colchester firm."

"Mmm – not now," he waved, staring past her at the TV.

Lucy turned and followed his gaze to the far wall of the staff lounge.

"What's going on?" she asked, acutely aware of the five p.m. deadline her clients had set.

"Everyone aboard the ISS is dead," said Myles, his eyes still glued to the screen.

"The ISS? As in the Int–"

"The International Space Station, yes," he snapped, his arms resolutely folded as he stared intently through his hipster glasses.

Lucy stopped scanning the room for other colleagues she needed to talk to, and started paying attention to the images on the TV.

A helicopter circled above a small black-brown capsule, which floated precariously atop the swell of the ocean. A naval rib, staffed with seamen in orange rescue suits, approached the floating cone-shaped object. As they drew level, the rescuers attempted to secure rope lines around the object.

They eventually succeeded and, once securely moored against the capsule, began to drill into its hull. They made swift progress. The helicopter camera zoomed in as the rescuers prised the hatch open. The opening was tiny, and its contents completely obscured from view by the lead rescuer, who was now leaning into the container.

He recoiled and shouted something to a colleague, who clearly disputed the information and approached the hatch opening himself only to similarly recoil in disbelief. The pair began to wave their arms, and one pulled out a radio. The camera zoomed out to reveal a US Navy frigate, which slowly tacked towards the bobbing pod.

"It's the Soyuz capsule," said Myles, without taking his eyes from the screen. "That charred cone. It was transporting the previous crew of the ISS back to Earth. But according to the news, NASA lost signal from the capsule during re-entry. Ah, come on!" he blurted, as the TV began to freeze up in pixelated glitches until the image distorted completely and the broadcast cut back to the newsroom.

"It was supposed to land in Uzbekistan or Kazakhstan or somewhere," Myles continued, looking at Lucy briefly, then back at the screen, "and instead it wound up in the Gulf of Aden, which is *not* near. Hey, here we go," he added, as the footage cut to an infographic charting the capsule's deviated course.

"What killed them?" asked Lucy, also now glued to the screen. "Have people ever died on the ISS before?"

"No," said Myles, "and they have no idea what did it. Apparently the whole station crew's heart rates plummeted during the night, and NASA have since lost all contact with the station. Or at least that's what the media's claiming."

"Email and internet's down for a while, people, sorry, soz, sorry," came the IT technician's voice as he whirred through the staff lounge in a hurry. "I'm gonna go reset the server so bear with me, and don't shoot the messenger, yada yada …"

"Oh great, well there goes the stock image library," said Lucy, mentally cursing as her five p.m. deadline slipped yet again.

"What was it you wanted?" asked Myles, finally peeling his eyes from the TV, which had moved on to a fresh story.

"It can wait now," said Lucy. "I'd better go phone the Colchester firm – and tell them their promo video's gonna be more like six p.m. at this rate."

"Where are they based?" queried Myles, as Lucy withdrew.

"London," she called over her shoulder. "They're pulling an all-nighter."

"Let me know if you get through," he persisted. "I had a teleconference scheduled with some clients there this morning, but we couldn't connect."

"Oh joy," said Lucy, rushing back to the office.

***

"Sorry I'm late!" chimed Lucy, bustling into the booth Cassie had reserved. She was definitely on the seven-thirty side of "seven o'clock". She took off her jacket and ran her hands through her long brown hair, which fell elegantly either side of her pale cheeks. The new sports bar was busy for a Friday night. "Maps wasn't working on my phone – no GPS signal or whatever."

"It's fiiiine," slurred Cassie. "I had problems with my cell earlier, don't take it personal, Luce." Cassie was halfway through an aggressively cheerful cocktail, and there was a suspiciously empty identical glass next to it. She laid her cracked smartphone out on the table. "It made me super late for a client appointment."

"Ever considered buying a case?" said Lucy, frowning at the splintered screen.

"Yes, Lucy, it's top of my to-do list – right after getting a boyfriend, a home, having kids, quitting my awful job, and stopping hating life," snarked Cassie.

"Glad you're taking that trademark optimism into your thirties."

"It served me so well in my twenties, why stop now?" drooled Cassie, taking another long drag through her straw. "Yes, I drank yours," she added, catching Lucy's glance at the empty glass. "You were late! What was I supposed to do, let it get warm? God, Luce, I'm not an *animal.*"

The waiter swung by.

"I'll have what she's having," said Lucy.

"Two cosmopolitans and a piña colada," replied the waiter, making a note.

"This is your third cocktail?" exclaimed Lucy, turning to Cassie. "I was only thirty minutes late!"

"Pff. 'Only.' Time is precious, Luce, gotta make the most of it. Besides, we Asians are famous for holding our liquor. That will do us nicely, thank you, good sir," she added, dismissing the waiter.

"Luce, your hair looks freakin' incredible. Oh my god, what do you use in it?" She almost threw herself over the table in a bid to reach Lucy's locks.

"OK great, so we're at the hair-smelling stage already."

"I may have had some pre-drinks," confessed Cassie, doing a small victory dance in the orange leather booth. "Hey, what's your news?" she buzzed, still dancing. "You said you had news, tell me! Oh my gosh, are you *pregnant*?"

"Am I what? No, I am *not* pregnant!" laughed Lucy.

"Then what is it?"

"Nothing – it can wait. Let's get you some nice starchy carbohydrates first, shall we?" said Lucy, reaching for the menu.

"Hey!" yelled Cassie, staring over Lucy's shoulder. "Hey! Fix your TV, man!"

Lucy turned and looked at the jittering sports screen. Large pixelated blocks stuttered across between blackouts, which was invoking disapproval from the bar's regulars.

"I don't think it's their fault, Cass – our TV at work was doing the sa–"

Cassie ignored Lucy completely, cutting across her.

"Do you even know how to run an establishment like this?" she yelled, grabbing a handful of salted cashews from the bowl on their table.

"Amen to that!" burped one of the balding men propping up the bar, turning and raising his beer in concurrence.

"I really hope you ordered those," said Lucy, regarding the half-eaten nuts with suspicion.

"One thing," said Cassie, shovelling cashews into her mouth. "All I wanted for my birthday was to see my best friend and watch the ball game, but can I even have that? No!"

"Hey, I'm here, right?" said Lucy, scooting round to Cassie's side and placing a consoling arm around her drooped shoulder.

"Meh," she shrugged. "Take it or leave it."

Lucy lifted the arm off and Cassie burst out laughing.

"Relax! I'm jerkin' you around. You're the best!" squealed Cassie, nearly wiping Lucy out with the force of her counter-hug.

The waiter recoiled just in time to save the new cocktails from annihilation, as he began serving up the fresh round.

"What's with your TV, bro? It sucks," said Cassie, turning her attention to the attractive waiter, and sliding Lucy's cocktail across with excessive speed.

"Sorry ma'am, we're trying to fix it. I think the satellite network's having some trouble, it's across all the channels," he replied, while Lucy dabbed spilt cocktail off her jeans.

"OK pal," replied Cassie. "I'll take your word for it, but only because you look like you were carved from freakin' candy." She reached out to stroke his face and the waiter swiftly backed away. Lucy mouthed an apology over her friend's shoulder.

"Uhhhhh! Are you shitting me?" said Cassie, slumping onto the table and burying her face in her arms with a groan.

"What?" said Lucy, looking around. Her eyes fell upon the door: Myles had just entered, with a girl. "Ah. Not ideal," she conceded.

"You see that bitch he's with?" mumbled Cassie from the table.

"Do you know her?" replied Lucy, surveying the petite blonde across the room.

"No, but she's a bitch."

"OK, we hate her, I'm cool with that," said Lucy, rolling her eyes and taking a substantial swig of cocktail. "You wanna go someplace else?"

"He's your boss, can't you just tell him to fuck off?" pleaded Cassie, turning her head to the side to peer out at Lucy.

"I think that's the last thing I can say to my boss, Cass," retorted Lucy, as the petite blonde took Myles's arm and laughed enthusiastically at some comment he'd made.

"Oh god, she looks about twenty! She's like half his age! Why is this happening to me?" whined Cassie, craning her neck out of their booth to get a proper view. "Shit!" She gasped, immediately ducking back down. "They saw me, didn't they?"

"Yes," replied Lucy.

"Are they leaving?"

"No," muttered Lucy, looking straight ahead with a fixed smile as Myles began to limp towards them. "They're coming over."

"Fuck! Fuck! This is *not* happening! No, no, no!" moaned Cassie, peering out of the booth again. "Wait, why is he even walking like that?" With that, she began to slide further down her seat until she was entirely submerged beneath the table.

"Cassie!" hissed Lucy. "Cassie, get up! You're being ridiculous! They're – *Myles!*" said Lucy, suddenly warming her tone and standing up to give her boss a cordial hug. "Long time no see! What's it been, forty-five minutes?"

"I think we could call it forty-six, but I won't split hairs," he replied with a chuckle.

"That'd be a first," came a mutter from under the table.

Myles rocked on his heels and hesitated, clearly debating whether or not to acknowledge the table situation. Lucy's throat began to dry with the awkwardness. Mercifully, Myles blinked first.

"Ah, Cassie," he said, striking an unconvincing tone of surprise. "I didn't see you there. How's it going? It's your birthday, right? Happy birthday."

"Leave it, Myles," huffed Cassie, clambering out from under the table to the genuine surprise of the petite blonde. "If there's one thing I learned over the past eighteen months, it's that birthdays mean jack to you. No wait, not birthdays, *people*. People mean jack to you."

Cassie swayed as she stood, prompting Lucy to put out a steadying arm, which Cassie gripped like the rail of a cruise ship.

"Perhaps we should be leaving," said Myles, his eyes darting away as Lucy tried to offer him a sympathetic smile through her own blushing.

"I'm Cassie," said Cassie, leaning into Lucy's by-now-restraining arm and scowling at the terrified blonde. "Did he ever tell you about me?"

"Um … no … but it's a pleasure to meet you, Cassie," said the younger girl, meekly extending a hand. "I'm Jennifer."

"Oh god," said Cassie, burying her head directly into Lucy's bosom. "Don't tell me she's *nice*. I can't handle *nice*." She spat the word like it was something dirty. "Lucy, I'm not equipped to deal with this situation, make it go away."

"Um," said Lucy, stroking her best friend's hair as Jennifer's hand slowly lowered.

"Wonderful to see you both," winced Myles.

"It's …" trailed off Lucy, also rendered socially constipated.

"No!" cried Cassie, straightening up again. "No, Myles. It's my birthday, so this time, I'm the one who gets to leave. Come on Lucy!" she said, pushing through Lucy's arm barrier and staggering away towards the exit.

"I should go catch her up – I'm so sorry," bumbled Lucy, but Myles waved a dismissive hand. "It was lovely to meet you, Jennifer. I hope you both have a nice evening. See you tomorrow, Myles."

He nodded, lips pursed in a painful smile. Lucy hastily pulled out some cash and left it on the table, knowing full well that Cassie wouldn't have paid for any of her drinks thus far, then set off after her drunken friend.

"What was up with his walk?" slurred Cassie, staggering down the sidewalk defiantly.

"Golfing injury, apparently," shrugged Lucy.

Cassie looked at Lucy incredulously. "What kind of A-hole injures themselves playing golf? Is that even possible?"

"Apparently, yeah."

"Ugh, who am I kidding, he still looked fantastic," whined Cassie.

Lucy kept quiet. She'd never understood Cassie's attraction to Myles. At a glance, the turtleneck made him look like a hipster, but in reality the man simply hadn't updated his wardrobe since the eighties. And he played golf.

"Worst. Birthday. Ever," grumbled Cassie, dragging her feet.

"Oh, I don't know about that," countered Lucy. "My tenth birthday was my first birthday without my mom. *That* was pretty sucky."

"Ah, cry me a river, heard it all before," dismissed Cassie.

"No siblings," continued Lucy, "a poor only child stuck on a Louisiana ranch, not realizing my dad was becoming an alcoholic …"

"Whatever, Luce, you had a terrible childhood. Give a crap?"

"I'd rather have a terrible childhood than your depressing-as-fuck adulthood," said Lucy, slapping Cassie playfully.

"You are such a jerk!" cried Cassie, laughing. "What would I do without you? Apart from all the way-cooler friends you're obviously holding me back from getting."

"Cassie, I actually do need to tell you something. My news – it's about my mom." Lucy reached out to her friend. "I found her."

"Wait, what? That's … I didn't even know you were looking for her! I can't believe you kept that from me!"

"I've kept it from Dan, too."

"Jesus Christ, Lucy, this is huge. Where is she?"

"Boston, apparently."

"*Boston*? I swear your family has some sorta allergy to staying still. How did you …?"

"I used an agency. They tracked her down. Took them a while – turns out she's changed her whole name. Calls herself Veronica now."

"Lucy, this is insane. Are you gonna go find her?"

"Don't know. Haven't really had time to think about it. I only got the letter a few days ago. They sent a follow-up email today asking what I want to do next, and I honestly haven't a clue."

"You have to meet with her!"

Lucy shrugged. "I'm not so sure. She was a pretty terrible mom. If I did, it would only be to ask her why she was such an asshole."

"It's like … your destiny!" breathed Cassie.

"Oh my god, you are so full of crap."

"Dan'll back me up on this. You're gonna tell him, right?"

"At some point. Just gotta find the right way. He's not the biggest fan of my mom. He's heard the stories."

"Lemme see the email," demanded Cassie.

Lucy retrieved her phone. "Sure, it's … Oh, great, now there's literally zero signal," she sighed, shoving the useless phone back in her pocket.

"I bet there's Wi-Fi in that place over there," said Cassie, pointing to a bar across the street, "which is perfect, because you look *really* thirsty. Come on Luce, your treat."

***

There was a knock at the door. Lucy checked her redundant phone: it was nearly one a.m. She'd only just got back in, after finally bundling Cassie into a cab. The bar (and the rest of the neighbourhood) had lost power, bringing Cassie's power-drinking to a fortuitous end, and allowing Lucy to enjoy a starry, sobering walk home.

Another set of knocks. Quietly, she got up from the kitchen bar stool and tiptoed towards the front door.

Lucy raised her eye to the peephole: it was pitch black in the corridor. A third set of knocks pounded the wood and she recoiled from the door with a gasp.

"Hello?" came a croaky female voice from outside. "Hello, mister or miss? Is Manuela from downstair. Hello?"

Lucy swore under her breath. She hadn't known the name, but there was definitely an older Hispanic woman living in the apartment below. Where was Dan?

46

Carefully, Lucy put the latch on the door and switched her phone flashlight on. She opened the door a few inches and shone the light out onto the uninvited guest. The old lady shielded her eyes, blinking, as Lucy scrutinized her from behind the door.

"Can I help you?" said Lucy, trying to check the hostility in her voice.

"Hello, miss. I am Manuela from 701. Sorry for waking you at this hour."

"No, no, it's OK, I was up," replied Lucy, dipping the flashlight slightly, and allowing Manuela to lower her hand.

"I am wondering please," the stranger continued, "if you have any water? Mine is not working. I try other apartment on my floor but no one is in, and I do not like the people downstairs, so I think: I try you."

"Oh, I see. Um, last I checked our water was off too," said Lucy, holding the door. The old lady didn't move, but stood and smiled expectantly.

"But, uh, I guess I can check again. Um, come in," sighed Lucy, removing the latch and opening the door properly. "I'm Lucy by the way." She extended a hand as the older woman entered.

Manuela shook it, graciously, then took her shoes off at the door. Lucy appreciated the consideration, but suddenly had a pang of fear that the old lady might be planning on staying for some time.

"The kitchen's right this way," said Lucy, leading her guest in. Lucy tried the main faucet but to no avail.

"Looks like we're still out," she said, with an exaggerated gesture towards the sink. "Are you thirsty?"

"My medication. I am need water for swallow my medication," replied Manuela, gesturing equally crudely to her mouth.

"Oh, I see. I think we might have some left in a jug," replied Lucy, reaching into the fridge. She pulled out Dan's jug of filtered water (now less than half full). It was already warmer than when she'd last drunk from it. "Do you have your meds here or should I put this in a glass?"

"They in my apartment. I borrow, if is OK? I return right away," suggested Manuela.

"No hurry," said Lucy, pouring much of the jug's contents into a glass, which she passed over to the woman.

"Thank you, dear," said the lady, standing up from the breakfast stool upon which she'd perched. "You very nice. Very beautiful young woman. I have no daughter. But I think I would like have daughter like you. Maybe in another life!" said the lady, with a soft chuckle as she wobbled back towards the door.

"Nice meeting you," said Lucy, holding the door open as Manuela carefully slipped her shoes back on. "Are you going to be alright getting back downstairs in the dark?"

"Si, si," said the old woman, stepping out into the hallway. "Of course. Thank you again, Miss Lucy."

The woman began to descend the stairs slowly. Lucy anxiously twiddled her cell phone in her hands for a moment then stepped out into the hallway. Pulling the front door shut, she caught up with Manuela in a few quick steps and offered the lady her arm, and some phone light, and escorted her slowly back to her front door.

When she got back in, Lucy took a deep breath and exhaled. *Be careful.* It had been the one thing in Dan's note that had really worried her. He wasn't the paranoid type. Still, he could hardly begrudge her helping a senior citizen with her medication.

Nonetheless, she deadlocked the door this time. She'd been so comfortable with darkness as a child, growing up in the middle of nowhere. But having spent the last third of her life in a city, she'd grown accustomed to the gentle light pollution of urban nights. Her comfort, it turned out, now depended on it.

As she sat back down in the bar stool, Manuela's compliments echoed in her ears. Lucy's mind couldn't help but wander to her own mother, somewhere out there in Boston. She fetched the letter from the agency and reread it for the hundredth time that week.

Retrieving a map of America from the bookshelf, she turned to Massachusetts. Prising the pages apart, she moved the flickering tea light closer to the map and looked upon the city, studying it intricately, and eventually poring over the roads that might take her there. She had to see her again.

The sound of a key scratching its way into the lock pricked her ears. It was almost two a.m. now.

"Luce?" came Dan's voice as the front door clicked open.

She shoved the envelope back into the drawer.

"Dan!" she cried, dashing out from the candlelit kitchen to her partner, who stood in the front doorway wearing a head lamp. "I saw your note," she quavered. "What the hell's going on?"

49

FOUR

Consignment

THE PRESENT – SUNDAY MORNING

"You coming or what?" snapped Dan, holding the front door open.

"Yes, chill out already!" replied Lucy, grabbing her keys off the sideboard.

"I don't want to get stuck with the lousy jobs," he grumbled. "The good ones'll go quick."

"You're assuming we'll get to choose what we're assigned," replied Lucy, closing the door behind them.

In the car home yesterday, KGO 810 had featured a state-sponsored infomercial: *Volunteer to get services back online, and earn extra rations. Report to City Hall from Sunday onward.* Given that she and Dan had failed to procure a gun, securing extra rations seemed a sensible second option. *Car travel strongly discouraged while signals down. All city buses now free of charge.*

They exited the gloomy lobby of their building.

"Look," said Lucy, pointing to a house on the opposite side of the street. A large poster had been crudely slapped over the brick wall.

CURFEW NOW IN EFFECT: DUSK – DAWN
SIREN WILL SOUND
REMAIN INDOORS
LETHAL FORCE WILL BE USED

At the foot of the poster were two smaller details:

By order of the Governor of the State of California.
Removing this poster is a criminal offence.

"*That* would explain it," said Dan, as a military patrol rumbled past, slowly. The soldiers glanced at the two of them with indifference as the jeep rolled over a set of disused tram lines. The heavy weaponry and uniforms were at odds with the clear blue skies above.

Yesterday's cacophony of horns had been reduced to an occasional beep this morning as drivers weaved more cautiously, the volume of cars more than halved. Lucy continued with Dan toward the bus stop where they found a dozen people already standing in line.

"Bus is gonna be busy," grumbled Dan.

Busy wasn't the right word. When the bus arrived it was fit to burst. The driver didn't even come to a halt; she just drove past them, raising an apologetic hand.

"Come on," said Lucy, giving Dan a nudge as she set off. "We can walk it. I think all the buses are gonna be like that. It's only a mile and a half to City Hall, no point going back for the car. We don't wanna waste any more fuel."

"Check out the school," said Dan, as they passed the local elementary.

Lucy surveyed the large truck parked outside. A pair of soldiers stood guarding the vehicle while two civilians hastily unloaded it.

"Must be the kids' rations," she concluded. "The radio said they'd be prioritizing schools."

"Mm," grunted Dan. "Good time to be a kid."

His strong arms swung as they walked. Breakfast had been modest, to say the least, and Lucy was getting the impression that just twenty-four hours in, her partner was finding the adjustment to rationing harder than expected. He was used to a muscle-building diet, and their new calorie budget was half that.

***

City Hall was worse than the buses. It was like a Major League baseball game with tens of thousands of people converging upon a single venue – only, City Hall was never designed to be a stadium. Long, snaking cordons had been set up to deal with the excess crowds, and there was a heavy police presence.

"I'll be honest," conceded Lucy, "I didn't expect this many people to show up."

"By the looks of it," replied Dan, "neither did the authorities."

It was two hours before the pair even made it inside the building.

"Thank you for your patience. Remain calm and you will be processed as soon as possible," repeated a police announcer for the hundredth time.

Each sprawling line continued to grow faster than the rate of processing. To Lucy's bitter disappointment, their entry into the hall only led to a further set of swollen lines, each edging forwards at a snail's pace. After a further hour of standing in the increasingly humid processing chamber, a large woman fainted and had to be helped to the side to recover. After that people began to sit on the floor and shuffle forward only when they had to.

Every now and then the sound of a baby crying would cut across the hubbub of the hall, setting off another infant, leaving the two wailing aimlessly while stressed parents tried desperately to placate them in the face of judgemental onlookers.

Finally, Lucy and Dan's turn came. The police officer controlling the front of the line signalled for Lucy to come forwards, which she did, but Dan was stopped short. "One at a time only!" snapped the officer.

Dan shrugged and retreated. Lucy continued towards the vacant kiosk alone.

"Name?" asked the desk clerk, barely looking up.

"Lucy Young."

"I need people in the following areas: power, medical, logistics, fire safety, and sanitation. Any preference?"

"Um … Can you be more specific?"

"No."

Lucy blushed. "Um, I'd quite like to stay with my partner. Can I ask him where he's going to choose?"

Again, the clerk barely looked up, giving a curt nod. Lucy hastened over to Dan.

"Power, medical, or logistics? Those are our choices. Pretty much," she added, filtering out the last two.

"Logistics – sounds least dangerous," replied Dan, decisively.

"OK. Make sure you choose the same," insisted Lucy.

She hurried back to the kiosk and stated her preference. The clerk wrote down some follow-up information, then tore off a slip and slid it across the desk to her.

"Take the exit on the right, show them this, and they'll tell you which bus bay to go to. You'll need to display it again when you get to work, so don't lose it. Next please!"

Lucy took the slip and moved towards the exit. She bent down and tied her laces, stalling for time until Dan had been processed and caught up. As they approached the exit together, a policeman barred their path.

"Tickets," he demanded, extending a hand. "You're this way, ma'am. Sir, you're coach seventeen," stated the officer, returning their papers.

"What? Wait, we're supposed to be together!" protested Lucy, holding up both tickets side by side.

"Sorry ma'am, you've been assigned to L4, and your partner's been assigned to L9."

"Then it needs to be changed."

"No transfers until the backlog's been cleared ma'am, sorry. You should be able to apply in a couple of days, though."

"Are you freaking kidding me?" she protested, prompting Dan to intervene.

"Sorry, officer, my partner's just tired is all. Is there really nothing you can do?"

"Sure, I can have you both locked up for the night? Or you can get the hell on with it like everybody else in this city and quit whining."

Lucy glared at the officer while Dan led her to the side.

"It's only for a couple of days," he said, looking her straight in the eye. "We'll be fine. It won't be like yesterday – the National Guard's on the streets now."

She nodded, acutely aware of the people starting to bunch behind them.

"Hey!" barked the officer.

"We're going, we're going!" replied Dan, hastily turning back to Lucy. "See you at home. Be careful."

They parted quickly and unsatisfactorily, without embrace or comfort. Lucy paced to coach L4 where the driver beckoned her to hurry aboard. She looked at the strangers lining each row, recognizing her own anxiety in a few of them. Grabbing the last empty seat, she craned to see out of the window – Dan was already gone. She took a steadying breath. Time to focus on the task ahead, whatever it may be.

***

"Bottles," said Lucy. "Refilling them. You?" she asked, stepping through the door.

"Inventory," replied Dan, coming through from the kitchen to greet her properly.

"You got Inventory?" she scoffed, incredulously. "That's your kind of OCD heaven!"

"Guess I lucked out. Lucky L9."

"Manage to pocket any Tootsie Rolls for us?" she jested.

"They caught someone doing that actually – stealing from the inventory. They beat him up pretty good. So I got us nothing. On the upside, none of my ribs are broken, so yay for that. How was bottles?"

"Best. Day. Ever. Oh no wait, it was terrible, because I was in a recycling factory."

"Just when I thought you couldn't get any sexier."

"You're right, it's pretty glamorous actually. I think I've finally found my calling in life," said Lucy, with a swish of her hair. "They want all the plastic bottles we can find to be cleaned for recirculation. It's a mess though; most don't have lids, and loads are split. I guess it's all part of the water rationing, but I really can't see how it's worth it."

"There was a flyer about it," said Dan, searching around. "It sorta makes sense, the way they explained it."

"Kinda, except that handing out and collecting bottles is super inefficient. Why not go around with a water truck and let people fill them up that way?" countered Lucy, eyebrow raised.

"Only angle I can think of is hygiene," mused Dan. "If people can't flush their lavatories, and water's rationed, then they're probably not washing their hands too often. Seems an easy way for people to get sick. Trust me, cholera's a much bigger problem than having you guys hunt around for bottles. I think I saw one of your water trucks on the route back, actually. It was stopped outside a retirement home."

Lucy inspected herself in the hallway mirror. "God I look like shit," she said, lifting her messy, matted hair up and prodding the bags under her eyes. "And I'm absolutely beat," she yawned, sitting down among the shoes in the hallway and pulling off her current pair. "I'd forgotten what it's like to stand up all day."

"Luckily for you we've got a gourmet dinner lined up," winked Dan. "Half a tin of tuna *each* plus a niiiice piece of bread."

"Truly, you spoil me," she snorted, extending a hand for him to help her back up.

"Nothing but the finest for my girl. Don't worry, we've got some relish left in the cupboard. And there's butter too."

The harsh, tinny sound of a voice amplified through a bullhorn echoed up from the streets outside. "Curfew is about to start. Return to your homes immediately," the announcement repeated on a loop.

Lucy wandered over to the glass balcony door and peered down as the patrol car passed by their street.

"Wow. They're not taking any chances on that one," she said, sitting back down and rubbing her feet again.

"Did you hear about the fire?" asked Dan.

"The fire?"

"Huge fire over on Southside, Hillsborough way. You didn't hear the sirens last night? Whole thing was nasty – apparently six people died. Someone had to drive to the fire station just to tell them their street was burning down. By the time the fire crew got there it'd spread to a whole bunch of other houses."

"Jesus. How come a patrol didn't spot it?"

"No idea. Makes you wonder, though, how good their patrols can be if they can't spot a street on fire at night-time."

"Is this the flyer?" asked Lucy, picking up a simple two-sided black-and-white leaflet from the table.

"Yeah, it was in front of our door when I got back. There was one in the mailbox too, actually. Pretty thorough."

Lucy scanned through the flyer. The design was extremely basic: pure information, no frills. *CIVILIAN GUIDELINES* read the title, under which were a short list of subtitles in smaller text: *Curfew, Rations, Schools, Buses, Employment, Safety.* She examined further.

CURFEW IN EFFECT DUSK TIL DAWN. SIREN WILL SOUND DAILY AT BEGINNING AND END OF CURFEW. STAY INSIDE. ARMY PATROLS WILL USE LETHAL FORCE.

RATIONS WILL BE DISTRIBUTED TO YOUR HOME WEEKLY ON GIVEN DAY BETWEEN 6-7PM. SOUTHSIDE ON WEDNESDAYS. NORTHSIDE* ON THURSDAYS. ALL CITIZENS WISHING TO RECEIVE RATIONS MUST BE PRESENT IN PERSON. NO EXCEPTIONS. STAND OUTSIDE YOUR HOME AND DO NOT MOVE. TRUCK WILL COME TO YOU. REPORT TO NEAREST HOSPITAL IF UNABLE TO SELF-PRESENT FOR RATIONS. YOU MUST MAKE YOUR RATIONS LAST SEVEN DAYS.

BOTTLED WATER WILL BE DISTRIBUTED EVERY 2-3 DAYS BY PATROLLING TRUCKS. LISTEN FOR ANNOUNCEMENTS. WATER BOTTLES ARE LOANS AND MUST BE RETURNED. NEW WATER WILL NOT BE GIVEN OUT UNLESS EMPTY BOTTLE IS RETURNED AT THE TRUCK. MAX. ½ GALLON PER PERSON PER DISTRIBUTION.

SCHOOLS REMAIN OPEN. CHILDREN WILL BE GIVEN LUNCH RATIONS AT SCHOOL, DAILY.

FREE DAYTIME BUSES WILL RUN ACROSS THE CITY.

VOLUNTEERS NEEDED TO HELP RESTORE UTILITIES. REPORT TO CITY HALL FOR ASSIGNMENT. YOU WILL BE PAID EXTRA RATIONS. AGE 16+ ONLY.

CONSERVE WATER. TAKE EXTREME CARE WITH CANDLES AND NAKED FLAMES. KEEP BUCKET OF WATER IN YOUR HOME TO TACKLE NON-OIL, NON-ELECTRICAL FIRES. IN EVENT OF FIRE, TRY TO EXTINGUISH FLAME, THEN EVACUATE ALL PEOPLE FROM BUILDING AND FLAG DOWN A PATROL FOR HELP.

At the bottom of the flyer was an asterisk, with smaller text:

*Northside defined as all homes north of Rivera street Westside and twenty-sixth street Eastside.

"Curfew in Effect. Extra Rations. Naked Flames. It's like a music festival, featuring the worst band names ever," muttered Lucy.

She reread the flyer, processing the information while chewing slowly, trying to stretch out the modest meal. She glanced across the table at Dan, who was doing the same, interspersing every mouthful with a small sip of water followed by a pause.

"I think they made a mistake with those flyers," he offered, after another slow sip.

"How so?" enquired Lucy, frowning as she turned the leaflet over in her hand, examining it more closely.

"The school rations. They shouldn't have mentioned them. Or maybe they shouldn't have done them at all," he continued, taking another micro-bite of tuna bread.

Lucy gave him a baffled look.

"There was a police car outside this school earlier," said Dan. "Saw it on the bus home."

"So?"

"I think it's to do with the rations."

"That's a bit of a leap," countered Lucy. "It could've been there for loads of reasons. Hell, if it was a high school, then it was probably for one of the kids."

Dan shook his head as he processed another bite.

"It was a middle school, and I think someone read that leaflet, or listened to the radio, and thought: 'Schools are getting a bucketload of free food? Every day? I'll have me some of that.'"

"You're saying someone robbed the school?" scowled Lucy.

"Food's the new currency, right? The government's paying us in it, so it must be. And according to this leaflet, schools receive large, daily deposits. They're basically unguarded banks now. This leaflet's just told every cynical person out there exactly where to go if they want a load of free food."

"You think people would actually do that? Steal from children? That's gotta be a minority of a minority, surely," pondered Lucy, unconvinced.

"A few hundred kid lunches are still at least one hundred adult lunches. I think from some perspectives, it'd be stupid *not* to do it. There'll be a lot of people who won't know how to make a week's rations last properly. And when they've run out of food by day four, who's gonna offer them more?"

Lucy considered this. "Aha – but you said money's pointless now. So even if a gang *has* lifted a load of kids' lunches, how are they gonna sell them if people have nothing to pay with?"

"I dunno. They'll pay with stuff, I guess."

"And if they don't have anything worth trading?"

"Welcome to the world of gang debt. You can't physically pay them, so they get you to do a favour for them instead – something pretty vanilla at first, but then say they deliberately overpay you in rations. You're greedy or desperate, so you accept, not realizing you're immediately in debt to them again, and the next 'favour' they get you to do is a little less savoury. And so on, and so on, until you're basically a hitman."

"Well that's depressing."

"Yup," agreed Dan, taking another sip.

"Thanks for the cheery dinner chat, babe. I'll think twice next time I borrow anything from you."

"They can fix it," declared Dan, setting his glass down. "You just keep the soldiers there while the kids eat. It'd slow delivery down, so I guess some kids would be eating at ten and others at, like, three, but at least they wouldn't get robbed."

A loud siren sounded from outside: a protracted electronic whine, lasting about four seconds. There was a pause of four more seconds then a second blast, followed by another pause, then the final siren.

"Holy crap that was loud!" exclaimed Lucy, removing her fingers from her ears. "That's gotta be the curfew alarm, right? Three seems excessive, surely?"

"Loud and clear is what it was," replied Dan. "If you're going to use lethal force, you gotta give proper warning. And that was pretty unmistakable." He took her empty plate and stacked it under his.

"We should go to sleep soon," said Lucy, watching her partner wipe the plates clean at a snail's pace. "You're tired, I can see it. I'm tired too. And we're eating less. We need to compensate by sleeping more."

"Sounds sensible," he sighed.

"Besides," added Lucy, her jaw creaking open into a yawn, "I wanna be on my peak game for the bottle factory tomorrow."

***

Lucy lumbered sleepily into the bathroom, feeling her way in the darkness, guided by the smell of bleach working hard. Once done, she made her way back towards the bedroom, only to pause mid-step, her ears pricked by the sound of an engine running outside and a car door slamming. She wandered over to the balcony and slid the door open as quietly as she could, stepping out onto the cold tiles. The moon was hidden behind cloud. Squinting at the dark streets below, she could make out a military truck at the bottom of the road. Its engine idled while the twin beams of its headlights illuminated the ground ahead.

At the edge of the light, figures moved in the darkness, weaving between rows of parked cars, occasionally ferrying something towards the truck before scurrying back into the shadows. Lucy watched for another minute, the bright headlights hampering her ability to focus on the dark peripheral figures. The secretive work continued until the last package was loaded. The last figure climbed back into the truck and it rumbled off up the street, soon disappearing into the next block.

Lucy slid the balcony door shut again and returned to bed, rubbing the pimples on her arms, quietly slipping into a claustrophobic dream.

***

"Assholes!" exclaimed a neighbour from the street below, slamming his car door closed and kicking his vehicle in anger. "Fucking *pirates*, the lot of you!" the man yelled, swearing at a passing patrol car before storming back into his home.

"Shit, so *that's* what they were doing," said Lucy, staring down at the irate man. "Are you seeing this?" She turned to look at Dan, who was engrossed in yet another ration count.

He came over to the window and peered down. More people were appearing on the streets, checking their cars – trying the engines, examining the fuel caps, and cursing loudly.

"None of the cars are working," he muttered, catching up with the situation.

"I saw it happening last night – I thought it might've just been a dream," said Lucy. "There was an army truck on our street for a while, then it went round the corner. It was really dark, I couldn't see much, but I'm guessing the next block's fuel's gone too."

She stared out at the commotion below. The people were stranded, powerless, and it made immediate sense. Cars were part of the city's bloodstream. The circulation of people kept the city alive, but that circulation depended on fuel – a fast-dwindling resource. So to keep its patient safe, the military would have to keep its heart rate slow and regular. "Mm," muttered Lucy, nodding to herself as she pieced it together.

"It's a control thing, surely," said Dan, rudely missing her entire internal monologue. "We're on track, by the way," he said, tossing a notepad and pen back onto the table next to their food stock.

"The thing I don't get," quizzed Lucy, "is how they knew which type of fuel they were extracting from each vehicle – because they all run off different gas, right? You think they've just mixed them all up? And how come our car alarm didn't go off?"

"The police definitely have ways to bypass car alarms, that's easy," reasoned Dan. "Dunno about the fuel, though. Maybe it was most efficient to collect it all then find some place to distil it apart again later?"

He looked at Lucy properly and his expression softened to one of concern. "You look pale."

"Gee, thanks."

"No, I mean – here," he passed her a vitamin bottle, "iron supplement."

She took it, gratefully, and necked a tablet before walking over to the calendar on the wall. Picking up a sharpie, she drew a large circle around the date.

"Happy day two of martial law, sweetie-pie," she said, as the pen squeaked across the vertical paper. "Ready for work?"

***

As they walked towards the bus stop for work, the chanting became louder.

"That doesn't sound too good," cautioned Dan, as they approached the main road.

Hundreds of people marched by, blowing whistles and chanting. A few had drums and air horns, to add to the cacophony.

"Where's our gas! Where's our gas!" rang the chant, over and over, as the people walked in the direction of City Hall.

A police patrol car slowly escorted the marchers, supported by three army jeeps at further intervals along the crowd. The soldiers eyed the protesters warily for signs that the atmosphere might turn. "Free! Movement! Is – a – right!" came a second chant, briefly overtaking the first.

"Are they insane?" gawped Lucy, watching as people shouted and marched as if they weren't surrounded by soldiers with machine guns.

"I'm not sure they've fully grasped the implications of martial law on their 'rights'," replied Dan. "People don't know what's good for them. It's precisely the reason they took our fuel away – these people can't see the bigger picture."

Lucy examined the people walking, looking for the usual protest markers – T-shirts with the anarchy symbol on, balaclavas, caricature masks of politicians – but these people looked exceptionally ordinary.

"I think this is about as grass roots as marches get," she said, as they stood at the periphery. "It looks pretty safe," she added, looking at the number of children in the crowd, following alongside their parents.

"Yup. And it could turn on a pinhead," said Dan, risk averse as ever. "Come on, let's find an alternate route. I can't see any buses coming this way soon."

***

When they met back at home that evening it was a quarter to six – nearly time for the north side of the city to receive its rations.

Lucy and Dan took their place outside their building. The street was lined with people anxiously awaiting food. Some made small talk, presumably those fortunate enough to have had well-stocked cupboards when the satellites failed. Others just stared blankly ahead, hunger sapping the conversation from them.

As she and Dan were new to the area they didn't recognize many of their neighbours, but Lucy spotted Manuela standing a few yards ahead, alone. Her shoulders were slumped. Lucy felt a pang, an urge to go over to the woman, but something stopped her.

"Everyone looks so anxious," whispered Lucy, putting Manuela to the back of her mind and trying to discreetly study the people on the opposite sidewalk.

"I don't blame them. You hear the rumours?" replied Dan, leaning in.

"I heard one at work," said Lucy, still observing the strangers ahead. "Folk were saying Northside's drop's been cancelled 'cos they ran out of food doing Southside yesterday. But I figured they were just talking trash, right?"

"I heard that too," said Dan, also scanning the crowd. "I'm pretty sure it's bull. But I also heard there was some commotion down at City Hall this morning."

"From the gas protest?"

He nodded. "Apparently things took a turn when the protestors reached City Hall. Some of them started demanding to see the mayor, then one person pulled a gun and that was that. Police took him out. Crowd panicked. Then there are like eight different versions of what happened."

"Tell me the version you believe."

Flashing lights signalled the arrival of the ration convoy, cutting Dan off before he could reply. Leading the way was a police patrol car, followed by an armoured vehicle, the supply truck, and a second armoured vehicle. From the cop's loudhailer came a sombre warning: "Move from your doorstep and you will be shot. Stay still. We will come to you."

People did not move from their doorsteps.

Efficient as the soldiers were, it felt like an age before they reached Lucy and Dan's building. Each recipient was stamped with an indelible date mark on their hand, giving them the air of inmates rather than civilians. Lucy's throat felt dry as she watched the preceding addresses take their parcels and disappear. Were there really going to be enough?

The truck rumbled forward to their building and stopped, the driver crunching on the handbrake but leaving the engine idling. The vehicle trembled, mirroring the unfed occupants of the street. Lucy eyed up the mounted gun turrets fearfully. She had never seen a machine gun up close before. Their abundance in movies and on TV was no preparation for actually looking down the barrel of one.

The soldier manning the nearby turret scanned the crowd. Lucy wondered if he'd had to use it yet. Being from the National Guard, he was probably local to the Bay area. There was a chance he'd have to train it on people he knew, people he'd grown up with, even. Could he go through with it, if it came to that?

"Hand," barked a soldier, who was suddenly standing in front of Lucy with alarming proximity.

"Uh," she stuttered as he grabbed her wrist and stamped it firmly, leaving a thin inky sheen on her skin. The man moved on to Dan, while a second soldier shoved a clear, thick plastic bag full of rations into Lucy's torso, which she narrowly avoided dropping.

The package was smaller than she'd expected. Her mind darted back to their table of rations in the flat and she felt her cheeks burn. What if other people knew? A group nearby were already discussing the size of the bags in less than positive terms. Dan had been right:

if anyone found out about their stockpile it would become a magnet as rations ran out. They had to keep their heads down.

The second armoured vehicle pulled level with them, its endless reams of ammunition poised to tear through row after row of delicate human tissue at the click of a button.

A face on the other side of the street caught Lucy's eye then vanished from view, obscured by the truck. Lucy gasped, craning her neck to try to see past the slow-moving vehicle.

"What is it?" said Dan, putting an arm around her shoulder.

The Humvee moved forwards, revealing the far sidewalk again.

"No, I ..." Lucy stared across the street at the groups of people retreating into their homes, searching for that familiar face. It had gone.

"Lucy?" pressed Dan.

"I ... I thought I saw Cassie, is all," she confessed. "But it must've been someone else."

"It's dark, easy to confuse faces. Cass'll be fine, Luce," consoled Dan. "She will have received her rations yesterday. I'm sure she's equally worried about you – and she needn't be."

Lucy nodded meekly, her brow wrought with concern.

"I don't know what the deal is with days off in our new 'jobs'," he added, "but when we get one, we'll go check up on her, OK?"

Lucy squeezed his hand in appreciation and they joined the whispering march of their fellow residents back into the building. As they climbed the stairwell, illuminated by an assortment of handheld flashlights, everyone fell into a slow, synchronized step until the crowd gradually thinned out floor by floor, with people quietly slipping into their abodes, away from further scrutiny.

FIVE

Medic

It was six days since the Northside ration drop. They'd managed to make their government-given provisions stretch the whole week, but only by supplementing them with food from their own supply on at least three occasions. Being underweight was not something Lucy's father had ever valued in a human being – it was "impractical and goddamned ungrateful", as he'd put it during her high-school crash-dieting phase. He'd been right, of course – a malnourished farm worker was no kind of worker at all; you needed strength to be useful.

Both she and Dan were still adjusting to the five-hundred-calorie reduction in their daily intake. Lucy flopped onto the bar stool that evening, kicking off her shoes and bringing her left leg up to rest across her right as she began to massage the ball of her foot.

"Long day?" called Dan from the bedroom.

Before Lucy could answer, the overhead lights flicked on, accompanied by the familiar clunk and hum of the refrigerator buzzing back to life.

"Oh my god!" she cried, jumping to her feet. "Oh my god!"

She marvelled at the ceiling lights as if seeing them for the first time.

Dan rushed through from the bedroom, a stream of joyful expletives tumbling out as he bounded towards her. The two jumped and whooped with unbridled glee.

"Phones!" he exclaimed, suddenly, rushing away to reunite his defunct device with a charger.

Lucy ran the other way and into the bathroom. "Oh sweet Lord it flushes, it *flushes*! And the shower's working too!"

"The TV stations are still down," called Dan from the lounge.

"Maybe they didn't know the power was coming back on?" said Lucy, joining him, breathless with excitement.

"Good point – I'll leave it switched to the news channel in case it comes back. Hey, do you think –" Dan paused, moving quickly over to the window and lifting the curtain back. "Luce, the street lights are back on! And look – people!"

The street lighting brought Lucy an overwhelming sensation of comfort. The muffled jubilation of neighbours above and below them resonated through the floorboards as Lucy took in the families and individuals dancing in their homes across the street, their rooms illuminated for the first time since the impact.

"Hello! Hey!" said Dan, waving emphatically at a family almost directly opposite them who were also at their window, taking in the phenomenon. They waved back, the kids jumping as they did so, everyone's usual social inhibitions and norms stripped away in the face of this overwhelming, unifying return to normality.

One of the kids stopped bouncing and began pointing to the right of Dan and Lucy. The girl's parents followed her gaze, their smiles faltering. Following the direction in which the child was pointing, Lucy's eyes tracked across the street and all the way to her and Dan's kitchen.

"Shit!" she cried, rushing through and hastily drawing the blinds closed.

"What?" quizzed Dan, letting the lounge curtain swing back into place.

"They saw our rations."

The innocent curiosity vanished from Dan's face. They'd let their guard down.

"How much did they see?" he asked, catching her up in the kitchen.

"All the packs on the counter. All the water. This cupboard door was open, so I guess all the tins in here. Fuck!" she cried.

Dan paced up and down. "This isn't good."

"No, no, it's OK," quavered Lucy. "The power's back now, so actually we don't need to worry. Right?"

Dan pursed his lips. "New rule," he decreed. "We keep nothing valuable in sight of the windows. Or the door, for that matter."

Lucy's shoulders dropped. "Agreed." She closed the cupboard and started to shift the gallons of water up against the wall, out of sight. "Hey – the radio should work now."

Dan seized the radio, flicking it on and immediately switching to longwave, scrolling until he found KGO 810. Somehow, it was still broadcasting. As he turned the dial up, bringing the babble into focus, it sounded like they were attempting an outside broadcast; the studio commentator's clear voice was being interspersed by terrible-quality audio from a number of interviewees, presumably passing by the street outside the studio.

"What do you think about the power coming back on?" asked the reporter on the ground.

"It's fucking amazing!" cried the random interviewee. "It's – I don't know, aaaah! We're back baby, we're back!"

"Yeah, and we gon' get *wasted!*" interrupted another, sending both into fits of laughter. "Party on the streets! Street-light party!"

"Street-light party!" echoed the first, laughing wildly.

"So you're planning on disobeying the curfew tonight?" probed the reporter.

"Fuck the curfew, the power's back yo', it's party time!" yelled the more excitable one. "Laters!"

"Laters!" repeated the other, as they disappeared out of the microphone's range, with diminishing cries of "Street-light partaaayyy!" cutting through the background hubbub.

"For those of you just tuning in," resumed the anchor, "you're listening to KGO 810. Our reporters are live on the streets of San Francisco, getting your reactions to the restoration of power. I'm going to remind listeners again of the statement we've received from the authorities, because it is somewhat different to the responses you're hearing on the street. And I ought to reiterate that the curfew has *not* been lifted, so please do not take risks. I know many of you will be excited tonight, but I would personally urge you to be cautious."

Lucy slumped down on a bar stool and faced the radio.

"The authorities," continued the anchor, "say they're 'proud to have achieved partial restoration of power', but are warning that the supply remains limited across California. So as I understand it, we'll be sharing the supply with other cities on a rotational basis. I'm told that City Hall is working towards publishing some sort of power timetable, to help citizens plan accordingly, but as it stands, I'm afraid that power will be supplied for two-hour periods only. I repeat, there'll be two hours of power, then that's it until the next round, folks. You heard it here first."

***

"It's the hydroelectric plants," declared Lucy the next day after work. "I heard one of the officers talking about it. They've managed to get some of them generating again, but they can only have so many plants online because they're on manual, which apparently takes like five times the number of staff, and we don't have enough people trained yet. Plus you need loads more people overseeing the actual grid distribution twenty-four seven to make sure the rotation's working. So yeah, fun fact: turns out automation was really friggin' useful."

"What about Diablo Canyon?" asked Dan, while prising open a ration tin. "Surely a nuclear plant's the obvious place to start?"

"No idea," said Lucy, "but that's probably because I work in a bottle factory, and only get my highly classified information through rumours and by flirting heavily with the military escorts."

Dan pulled a less-than-impressed face and returned to his unedifying meal.

"Oh relax, jeez!" she chuckled. "I'm only kidding. If it's any consolation, I picture you every time."

"You're the actual worst. What if I've got some sexy army mistress down at the depot? For all you know I could be having dozens of wild affairs in the warehouse."

"I think we both know that the thing turning you on in that warehouse is the neat, orderly rows of itemized boxes."

"Nothing wrong with that," winked Dan.

"There are a couple of things, actually."

"Hey, can you imagine what this is gonna be like come winter? We'll be OK, but what's it gonna be like for some place like Chicago if there's still no power?"

"I imagine they'll do what people in Alaska are probably doing right now. Burn things," replied Lucy, bluntly.

"Sure-fire way to lose the deposit," Dan retorted, looking around the apartment.

"I could go for some fire-making. It'd be … nostalgic. Relive the glory years of a misspent youth."

"I hate to break it to you, Luce, but when people say 'misspent youth', they normally mean they wasted it playing video games or something, not cattle ranching. That's called 'child labour'."

"Yeah, but it means come winter, I'll be the one making us a mean bonfire," she grinned back. "Although my source at the bottle factory informs me it'll all be fixed by next week," she added, cracking open a tin of tuna from the cupboard, "and so far he's only been wrong one hundred per cent of the time. Dinner?"

***

Another three days passed before their city's turn for power came up again. The only places receiving electricity regularly – according to Lucy's ever-reliable source – were the hospitals and prisons. Food was concerning her more, though; yesterday's State-given ration pack had felt lighter than the first, something confirmed by her neighbour's faces.

That afternoon, however, had brought some relief: it was "payday" for all City Hall employees. Shifts finished early and workers were bussed back to City Hall to collect their bonus rations in person. It also meant Dan and Lucy could take the second bus home together.

The evening was mild – in the two weeks since global satellite failure, temperatures had risen to several degrees higher than normal for mid fall. As they walked homeward, back up their steep road and away from the bus stop, ration parcels tucked under their arms, a gentle tide of feathery seeds danced in the wind – like dandelion seeds, only with a golden hue.

Lucy tracked a twirling seed until it drew her eye to an elderly man across the street. His stooping frame was adorned by a long trench coat which he held together tightly at the collar, his other hand securing a dark blue woolly hat atop his head. His steps were small and unsteady. As the bus pulled away behind them, disappearing behind the next block, the sound of the man's coughing became louder and more violent until suddenly he fell to his knees, collapsing forwards onto his frail torso, his entire body convulsing on the ground as each retching cough gripped him.

"Oh god!" exclaimed Lucy, watching the man fall.

A young couple nearby ran to him.

"Somebody get a doctor!" cried the young man, as he and the woman rolled the elderly patient onto his back.

"You go to them – I'll get help!" cried Lucy to Dan, and she ran towards the intersection. She scanned the street in both directions – there was a patrol vehicle, but it was driving away from their block.

"Hey! Hey, help!" she yelled, desperately jumping and waving her arms. She began to sprint after the truck, continuing to shout, until one of the soldiers heard her. The patrol stopped in its tracks and turned around. "Help!" she shouted again, urgently beckoning them to follow.

The patrol quickly caught up and radioed for an ambulance, while Lucy returned to Dan's side. She stood only a yard from the old man's feet, watching in horror as the first couple on the scene tried desperately to resuscitate him. The patient's white hairs rippled gently as the strangers pummelled his ribcage. It cracked loudly under the compressions. The woman pinched the old man's nose and tilted his chin back, unflinchingly placing her mouth on his and trying in vain to revitalize him with secondary oxygen at set intervals. But each time, his inanimate head simply lolled to the side, his mouth hanging open, as if beckoning to his dislodged blue hat a few inches away.

The two soldiers stood back from the fallen man and watched as the civilians continued their attempts to save him. The sound of the ambulance's siren approached and Lucy felt Dan's hand on her wrist.

"We need to get indoors, now," he said, quietly, pulling her away from the scene and back towards their apartment. "I'll explain inside."

Lucy worked to keep up with him as he climbed their stairwell at speed, taking it two steps at a time for the entire eight floors. Her mind was fixating on the image of the fallen man; they'd witnessed the life force vanish from his body, sending his frail, discarded shell crashing to the ground. The last she saw was the ambulance crew scooping him up onto a stretcher and loading him into the back of the vehicle – while the other couple watched on hopelessly.

"Did you see the paramedics?" panted Dan, taking the apartment key from his pocket as they reached the eighth floor. Even in the short bouts of power, he refused to let them take the elevator, insisting that it wasn't worth getting trapped. At least the stairwell lights were working. "Luce?" he persisted, opening the front door and stepping into their illuminated apartment.

"What? Oh, uh, yeah?" she said, hastily refocusing as she followed him inside.

"They were wearing face masks," he said.

"OK," replied Lucy, pulling off her shoes.

"Think about it. What else was wrong?"

"An old guy just dropped dead in the street, Dan. I'm gonna say that's pretty fucking wrong," she snapped.

Lucy felt him place a gentle hand on either shoulder. She lifted her chin and looked him straight in the eyes.

"Luce, I'm not being flippant. This matters," he insisted. "Think about what we just saw, and think about what didn't stack up. Where were the military?"

"They –" Lucy paused for a moment to think, then began to re-evaluate what she'd seen. "They stood back from the old man – away from him. They didn't help the couple trying to save him."

"Good. What else?"

"The paramedics were putting him into a body bag. They didn't even try a defibrillator or anything – they just decided he was dead."

"Right," said Dan, relaxing his arms and rubbing his cheeks. "So we both saw the same things and I'm not losing my mind. That's something, then, at least."

"Why, what do you think it means?" pressed Lucy.

"I think it means they made two assumptions: one, they knew his death was a foregone conclusion, which itself means they probably know what killed him. Two, they know it's contagious, which is why they had masks, and put him straight into containment, and the military knew to stay several yards away."

"But if they know what he died of," considered Lucy, fast-forwarding through events all over again, "then that must mean other people have already died of it?"

Dan reached into a kitchen cupboard and pulled out two face masks, similar to the ones the ambulance crew had been wearing. "From now on, we wear these at all times outside of the house."

"Seriously?" balked Lucy. "Where did you even get those?"

"I told you – the night the satellites went down I bought everything I could think of. This is something I thought of."

"Dan, how will we eat?"

He finished fitting one of the masks to his face. "I don't know." His voice was slightly muffled. "We'll figure it out."

He held out a mask for Lucy to try on. She looked at her partner, who had in one fell swoop transformed into a surgeon: his mouth and nose covered, all the emotional information vanishing from his face, the only remaining clue being his eyes. As she pulled the elasticated bands of her own mask down over her hair, she felt distant from him. Sealed off from the intimacies and nuances of her partner's lips.

"It fits but I don't like it," she said, taking hers off.

"Me neither." Dan removed his too. "And mine's already sweaty, which I'm pretty sure kinda ruins them."

"How d'you know it's contagious, whatever took the old guy down?"

"I'm guessing. But if the medics are wearing them, it's a safe bet. Dad hinted something like this was coming. A pandemic of sorts."

"Wait, but – is it to do with that yellow stuff that was on the ocean? I don't think anyone's ever seen that before."

Dan nodded.

"And you didn't think this was worth mentioning before now?"

"I wasn't sure it was ever going to happen!" countered Dan. "We've had enough to deal with without worrying about some other unknown. Dad only mentioned it towards the end of the call, then we got cut off, so I couldn't find out more. He said something about possible contamination from the ISS, but that it was speculative. Honestly, Luce, this was a footnote in the conversation I had with him – it was all about getting rations and preparing for martial law. This scenario didn't feature highly."

"But now you've decided it's definitely happening?"

"You saw for yourself! Yellow scum, weird golden seeds, the military staying back, the medics not even trying to save the guy. When have you ever seen any of those things?"

Lucy didn't have an answer, and instead paused to consider.

"So," she replied after a moment, holding up her mask, "what do we do with these then? If it's in the air, we need to wear them all the time, right, otherwise what's the point?"

Both of them stared at their masks, unwilling to accept the obvious logical truth. It was plain to Lucy that neither of them wanted to be wearing the masks at all, let alone in their own home. After some contemplation, she pulled hers back over her face with purpose.

"Twenty-four hours," ventured Lucy. "If it's airborne it'll spread fast. There'll be announcements – or bodies. If it's not airborne, then we can take these off at the end of the day."

Dan pulled his on too. "Agreed."

***

When they awoke the next morning, the air was thick with spores. It was like a blizzard, only instead of snow, the haze was comprised of floating seeds, giving it a mustardy hue. Lucy looked at Dan with concern as the two stepped out of their lobby and into the gentle storm, each wearing their protective mask. Lucy put their umbrella up immediately, shielding them from much of the onslaught. Other figures appeared through the haze, some also using umbrellas, although none wearing masks.

As she and Dan reached the bus stop, the wind died down, and the visibility improved slightly. The spores formed a soft, springy layer underfoot, giving the sidewalk a cushioned quality.

"This is my bus," said Dan, through his mask. "Are you sure you're gonna be OK?"

"Yes. Are you?"

"Yeah. Promise me you won't take your mask off," he said, as the bus doors opened.

"I promise. Same goes for you," she replied, grabbing him in a hug before he boarded the bus. Its windscreen wipers pushed squashed seeds from side to side as the packed vehicle pulled away. Lucy turned and surveyed the streets around, trying to process the new sepia blanket that covered everything from the tar to the roof of the bus shelter.

Her bus came, some time later. Lucy stared out of the window as they drove; every soldier they passed wore a face mask. Even though the danger in the air outside was visible, she still had to fight the burning urge to rip her mask off as the temperature on board rose with each new wave of workers that got on. A permanent layer of condensed breath had formed a stifling microclimate on the inside of the white shield. Humid droplets now precipitated from the semi-plastic membrane above her nose back down onto her captive lips.

The day was long, her every thought dogged by concerns of hygiene; each second was but another opportunity to be infected by a colleague, by her food, by the very air she couldn't help but breathe. Her co-workers asked one after another what the mask was for, but Lucy ignored them, wishing neither to invite further conversation nor to risk someone stealing her only form of protection. She couldn't tell if it was her paranoia, or if her colleague down the line was developing the same rattling cough as the old man, but she kept her distance.

When finally the time came to return home, it became clear the situation had worsened. Fresh bodies lay scattered along the streets, this time not just the elderly, but the young too. Most were surrounded by concerned onlookers either trying in vain to help or attempting to flag down other passers-by in their panic. As the bus drove Lucy began to count the bodies.

"Six bodies," she muttered beneath her mask, shaking her head. "Six in five minutes." And zero ambulances.

Lucy's bus came to a premature halt and the doors opened. She craned her neck to see the owner of the heavy footsteps that reverberated up each of the bus's metal steps. A sergeant appeared, a white mask covering the lower portion of his face. He said something brief to the bus driver then turned to the passengers, megaphone in hand. The sergeant's amplified tone was brisk and assertive, cutting through the mask's muffling effect.

"You are each about to be issued with a face mask. You must wear it at all times. If you know someone who is sick, do not allow them to remove their mask. Do not allow yourself to come into contact with another person's bodily fluids. Remove your mask only when you need to eat and drink. Do not swap masks with anyone else. And do not lose your mask; as of this moment, your mask is your life."

With that he departed the bus, to the shock and confusion of the murmuring passengers on board. Their voices quickly mounted into a wall of noise and fears into which a lower-ranking cadet entered, hastily throwing two masks into each row as he traversed the length of the vehicle, not stopping to answer any questions and strenuously avoiding all eye contact. He was off in less than a minute. The doors of the bus closed once again and it pulled away, passing through the makeshift checkpoint that now stood barring the road.

When Lucy's stop came, Dan was waiting for her.

"How come you're here?" she said, embracing him fiercely as she stepped across the slushy, trampled seed carpet of the sidewalk.

Dan clung to her just as intensely.

"I checked the apartment and you weren't there, so I figured I'd come wait for you. I guess I was anxious. And –" He hesitated. "I guess you saw on the bus back. The walk isn't gonna be the nicest."

Lucy nodded, taking his hand as they set off homeward in the fading light. When they arrived, dotted along their street were three bodies, spread at large intervals. They weren't sprawled like the old man's had been; rather, they had been neatly placed parallel to the edge of the sidewalk. Fresh spores were already settling on top of them.

"Let's get in," said Lucy, picking the pace up. They reached their darkened building as a family of three were leaving. They were in a state of distress, carrying a smaller, fourth body between them.

"I'm sorry," said Dan, casting his eyes downward as he held the main door open for the group. Lucy stepped to the side, unsure what to do with her hands as the mourners passed. Once the group was clear, she and Dan furiously wiped their shoes on the building mat, removing any traces of seeds.

Dan took out his flashlight as they began to climb the unilluminated stairwell. Lucy's footsteps echoed with his, falling in and out of time with each other, until Dan suddenly froze mid-stride, throwing out a hand behind him to stop Lucy from advancing any further. He faced straight ahead. They'd reached the sixth floor, where a hacking cough above them was growing louder and louder.

"Can you see who it is?" whispered Lucy, trying to project from behind her mask without being detected by the floor above.

Dan shook his head, still rooted to the spot with his arm outstretched, dipping their flashlight. Looking up ahead, Lucy watched as streaks of light from the unseen stranger jerked around erratically. The coughing continued, escalating into almost barking. Lucy shuddered at the victim's pain, palpable as it was in the sound of delicate lung tissue deteriorating amid bronchial spasms. Cries of pain and gasps for air punctuated the disturbing overture as it reverberated around the hallway. Finally, the crumpling thud of a body hitting the ground signalled it was over.

"I think they're dead," whispered Dan, the whites of his eyes flashing as they darted between Lucy and the ascending spiral of stairs. "Christ."

"We have to get past, we can't stay here forever," she whispered back. "And if they're still alive, then we need to call an ambulance."

He looked back at her and hesitated.

"*Dan*," she hissed, urgently.

"Alright!" he whispered back harshly, before turning and slowly continuing upwards. As they rounded the lip of the seventh floor, he froze again. Lucy gasped as she too saw Manuela's outstretched body. Bloodshot eyes protruded from her skull, goggling from the exertion of death. The rest of her body was twisted and contorted, lasting evidence of the pain endured. The door to her apartment stood closed behind her, unmoved, the key still clasped in its owner's mottled hand. Around Manuela's other hand was the ribbon attached to her flashlight, which sent a now-steady beam of light across the far wall.

"She *looks* dead," said Dan, reaching out then recoiling – clearly too afraid of contamination to risk taking a pulse.

"Manuela?" asked Lucy, tentatively, afraid the corpse might spring back to life with renewed spluttering and rasping. But Manuela just lay there, gone.

"We can't leave her like this," said Lucy. "We need to move her."

"Agreed," Dan replied, not moving.

His eyes were fixed on the victim's face, and Lucy couldn't help but copy. Both of their brains stalled, as if forcing them to process the level of anguish contained within each burst capillary, each fraction of an inch that the woman's eyes had edged forth from their sockets. Lucy and Dan had now directly witnessed two people being killed by the disease, and Lucy could only assume the bodies she'd seen from the bus had all suffered the same violent death.

"Move her," said Dan, snapping out of the trance. "We need to get her onto the street immediately. The contagion's still in her body. If it was affecting her lungs, then it's in the air here too."

"Yes. Right," replied Lucy, startled by the callousness of her own subconscious as it wandered through the closed apartment door and to the glass Manuela had never returned. She hadn't had to confront death like this in a long time. She'd forgotten what it did to the mind.

The two of them carefully stepped over the body and continued up to their dark apartment, where they immediately lit the kitchen candle. Putting on vinyl gloves, they picked up a small stack of trash bags to wrap the body in, and Dan swapped his regular flashlight for his head lamp.

Lucy wrote a note with Manuela's first name, address, date, and her approximate time of death on it – as well as the suspected cause of death, which she simply put as *virus*. They returned to the body, which was exactly as they'd left it, and Lucy taped the note to Manuela's blouse. She was about to close the lady's eyelids, but Dan stayed her hand.

"Don't," he said, grabbing her wrist in time. "The contagion could be in her fluids, like the guy said on the bus. It'll be on her eyes."

Lucy nodded, and the two of them began negotiating the body into the first trash bag.

"What should we do with her flashlight?" said Lucy, carefully unravelling it from Manuela's wrist.

"I don't know," said Dan. "Could it be infected?"

"We could bleach it? I'll leave it next to her door," decided Lucy, switching it off, "in case we need it in an emergency."

They continued to package the body, first getting the legs into one bag, then the top half into another, before taping both bags together where they overlapped in the middle.

"I'll go first," said Dan, swivelling the body round so the head was just protruding over a lower step. They carried her body as carefully and respectfully as they could down all seven flights of stairs, but it was hard going. They had to stop on multiple levels just to catch their breath and wipe the sweat from their brows. Lucy couldn't believe how heavy the corpse was. In the back of her mind she wondered what a stranger would say if they happened to find them like this, but her question was answered when they got outside. Coming out from almost every house on the street were groups, mostly twos and threes, all accepting the same terrible task that had befallen them – bringing the dead out on to the street.

Some bodies were wrapped in makeshift shrouds of bed sheets and blankets. Others were completely unchanged, simply being carried in the clothes they'd died in. The one thing all the bodies had in common was the same contorted signs, the same telltale cause of death writ across their twisted, violent final postures: their deaths had been sudden and brutal.

Many of those carrying the bodies were heartbroken, their cries muffled by the masks over which tears now streamed, rolling down onto each mourner's chin and off into nowhere. Lucy's mind flashed to southern Louisiana, to Clinton, her childhood community. Were they suffering in the same way? Were her friends from Wisconsin U, now scattered across the country, all caught up in the same awful predicaments? She wondered how many of them were carrying bodies now, who of them was crying, who would be putting on a brave face, who might be the first to die.

Unsure what else to do, they lay Manuela's body out on the sidewalk as others had done, parallel to the road.

"Feet," said Lucy as they returned to the building. She stopped in the entrance and scraped the spores off the soles of her shoes with repeated, heavy drags across the rough mat. Dan did the same.

A lone man overtook them as they reached the stairs, hurrying up to his second-floor home, locking the door behind him loudly as if doing so might offer better protection against the invisible disease.

As they reached the eighth floor, the main lights came back on. Neither of them said anything.

***

The curfew alarm sounded as Dan re-entered the bedroom, holding one towel around his waist while pressing another into his dripping hair. They'd both seized upon the narrow window of electricity that had opened up shortly after they'd returned home. Lucy had gone first and was now enjoying the luxury of a hairdryer, its warmth gradually offsetting the bracing cold of the shower water. Dan said something unintelligible through his mask, so she paused the dryer.

"You sure you're OK?" he repeated.

"Yeah … it's just … bad memories, that's all," she replied.

"Your dad?"

Lucy nodded. "Not been that close to a dead body until today, which is a good thing, I guess. Well, yesterday if you count the old man."

Dan gave her a sympathetic shoulder-squeeze as she resumed her drying by the window. She peered out at the street below, at the lame cars partially illuminated by the light spilling out of the lower-floor apartments. This was the first time the power had been on after curfew, and the city authorities had cut the street lights. Perhaps they were seeking to avoid any conflicts of interest, thought Lucy, or perhaps they wanted to hide what was happening.

"Dan," she said, calling him over.

He came over to the window, and the two of them watched as a pair of masked soldiers climbed out of a truck and began retrieving the bodies lining the street. The pair struggled under the weight. One soldier tripped against the sidewalk and dropped his half, fumbling immediate attempts to relift it as his partner continued dragging the body.

There was no ceremony about it; the soldiers were rushing. Lucy quickly counted the number of bodies left on the darkened street and extrapolated an average death toll for their block: thirty, at least.

As the truck pulled away, it joined a convoy of similar trucks passing down the adjacent main road. She considered how many streets there were in San Francisco, and how many people might be dying on each one that very moment.

They took advantage of the power to tune into KGO 810 again. A different presenter's voice filled the airwaves, her soft tone at odds with the chilling confirmation that the pathogen or toxin – no one knew quite what it was yet – was airborne. The presenter stated that people were linking the deaths to the newly appeared spores, although this had not been scientifically verified. However, the report did confirm that the spores were originating from the yellow scum covering the beachfront.

"Symptoms of infection include prickly skin, fever, dizziness, seeing bright spots, blurry vision, and sweating," said the anchor, dispassionately. "If you think you're developing symptoms, quarantine yourself immediately. Stay away from people and pets until twenty-four hours have passed. If you're still alive after twenty-four hours, then you're likely to be OK," she added, an unmistakable tone of doubt creeping into her voice. "If you do have the virus," continued the presenter, "it will likely kill you within three hours."

"That's not especially encouraging," remarked Dan, busily counting the rations again.

Lucy listened until the news was finished, then turned the radio off.

"You hear that last bit?" she asked Dan. "We have to report to City Hall again – for reassignment."

"What I don't get," said Dan, ticking off a stack of tins, "is why you have to quarantine yourself for twenty-four hours, if the disease kills you within three?"

Lucy considered. "Maybe symptoms come on slower in some people? Or it could be the incubation period?" she mused. "Like, you could end up accidentally killing someone within the first twenty-one hours if they don't have the same natural resistance as you. That's almost certainly why they've closed the schools."

"I remember when I was growing up," ruminated Dan. "If one kid got sick, everyone had it within a week."

"Maybe that's why we're being reassigned – that's gotta be thousands of parents who now have to stay home and look after their kids. Quite a hit to the workforce."

"Maybe," replied Dan. "Or maybe it's because the workers have started dying. We've had people dying on my job – I guess it's the same at yours? Maybe the State knows where this is headed?"

As she lay in bed next to Dan later that evening, staring up at the ceiling, she repeatedly resisted the urge to adjust the mask on her face, hyper-aware of the elastic digging into the skin beneath her ears. The goggles covering her eyes were no better; Dan had insisted they wear them too now that they knew the disease was airborne, but each new layer of protection only made her feel less secure.

Her eyes eventually grew heavy. Her mind wandered to an old childhood memory of her parents arguing. She was in her small bed, clutching her favourite teddy bear, and singing to it to try to block out the shouting. She couldn't see either of her parents, they weren't in the room, but the walls of the house were like paper, and her father's voice carried. She couldn't remember what they were arguing about, so her mind invented nonsense conversations instead. Angry, muffled syllables invaded the four small walls. Footsteps approached in a hurry. Her bedroom door flew open, setting the bells on the handle jingling.

Her mother ran to Lucy's bedside and scooped her up, carrying her out into the corridor. Lucy squinted, remembering how bright the hall lights had felt. Her father's voice continued to yell incoherently, closer now, as her mum carried her through the house and out to the car. "She's coming with me!" cried her mother, as she lowered Lucy into the passenger seat. Lucy pressed a hand to her cheek then pulled it away; it was wet and black with her mother's running mascara.

Her mom turned on the ignition, but the car wouldn't start. She tried again, and again, to no avail. She turned to Lucy. "Mommy'll be back in one minute, my baby," she said, and got out of the car, closing the door behind her.

Lucy blinked and opened her eyes. Her heart was racing. The room was darker now. She had no idea how long she'd been asleep for, but the dream had been vivid. The argument in it had been real enough – such fall-outs had been daily, right up until her mother left.

But her mom had never tried to take Lucy with her. And in that moment, in the darkness, after twenty years of living without the woman, it hurt like hell.

Dan lay stretched out next to her, a million miles away, lost in his own thoughts and fears. Lucy moved her hand over to meet his and squeezed it, hard, holding on with no intention of letting up. He reciprocated, sleepily, and rolled over towards her.

"Are you OK?" he mumbled.

"Yeah," she said, squeezing her eyes shut and taking a deep breath, stemming the tears that were pooling in her goggles. She quickly flipped both lenses up a couple of millimetres, allowing the salty water to drain away down her cheeks.

He gently raised his hand to her face. "You're crying," he said, softly, and scooped her up in his arms, his mask resting on her shoulder.

She clung to him, scared that her present was slipping away from her, scared that her past was catching up with her, and terrified that she was experiencing every symptom of the disease at once.

She focused on regulating her breathing as waves of anxiety smothered her. The radio report began to play over and over in her mind. She searched for solace, trying mindfulness, distraction, anything and everything she could to lower her pulse and alleviate the crushing sensation across her chest. Finally, a single thought allowed her sleep: if either of them was infected, they'd both be dead by morning, and the fear would be over.

SIX

Containment

Lucy glanced across the breakfast table at Dan, who wasn't eating either. Like her, he was hesitating to remove the protective mask. She stared out of the window, transfixed. The sky rippled with mustard-yellow spores drifting in the wind. Lucy's larynx twitched in aversion.

"We need to make this apartment airtight," declared Dan from behind his mask and goggles. "Otherwise we'll starve trying to avoid infection."

She considered their building's composition: it was about thirty years old, so built to a pretty decent standard. The balcony, on their one external wall, was covered in around half a foot of fluffy seeds. Those could be swept off, she figured. It would be a matter of sealing all the windows and doorways, and meticulously checking for cracks in the floors or walls.

"We'll need a vent, though, with a filter, right?" She cast her eyes around the rest of the kitchen. "And we'd need to block the sink —

all the drains, really. Which means no more showers or toilet flushes when the power's on."

Dan nodded, following her gaze. "We can find workarounds. Wash up in a bucket and empty it on the street, stuff like that."

"You mean shit in a bucket, don't you?"

"Hey, I'm fully open to alternatives, but yeah, it's looking that way. Blocking the drains should be doable. We've got some silicon sealant in that cupboard. Reckon that'd be enough to hold the plugs in place?"

"Maybe. What about the overflow holes? Could we get away with just taping over them?"

They set to work, starting with the drains, sealing them up one by one – even sealing off the faucets too after turning off their water supply entirely. It was all or nothing, she told herself: either you eliminated every possible risk of airborne contamination – including the small amount of air pumped through with every turn of a faucet – or you threw it all away. One weakness in your whole plan, and that would be the flaw that killed you. Besides, for the time being they still had Dan's largely untouched stockpile of water, which they'd been able to replenish during sporadic bouts of power.

Once the faucets were sealed, which didn't take long, they commenced the larger operation of sealing off the rest of the apartment. They began with the obvious suspects: windows, window frames, and balcony doors, sealing them with a combination of heavy-duty duct tape and dust sheets from their recent move. Within a couple of hours the apartment resembled a crime scene. The plastic sheets covering the balcony doors thrashed back and forth with each fluctuation of the wind outside, crackling loudly.

"Shit," said Dan, placing his hand to the side of the door. "You feel that?"

Lucy copied, and felt a light breeze tickle her palm. She thumped the wall in frustration. "Goddamnit!"

It wasn't airtight. They assessed the situation, looking for their mistake.

"What if we sealed them from the outside?" suggested Dan, pointing to the balcony doors. "We could climb out through the kitchen window?"

"And let a bunch of those seed things in while it's open?" frowned Lucy. "No way. Besides, we'd have to step in them too, and open the window again to get back in. Too much of a risk."

With no better alternatives available, they added a second layer of shrink-wrapping to all of their windows and doors, double-taping the seams this time.

By early afternoon they had double-sealed off everything apart from the front door. And yet it was all moot if they couldn't address two remaining problems: the issue of creating a filtered air vent, and creating an "airlock" so that they could enter and exit the apartment without compromising it. They sat in silence for a minute, contemplating the next step. Dan's stomach groaned loudly; it had been sixteen hours since their last meal.

"My work!" exclaimed Lucy, her eyes all lit up. "How did I not think of it before?"

Dan looked nonplussed; the connection to her advertising job clearly wasn't jumping out at him.

"We were filming a commercial – before the satellites failed," she elaborated, "and the cast were in hazmat suits. I think the suits are still at the office!"

Dan's eyes lit up. "Are you sure they were real? They weren't just props?"

"No, they're real! We got them on loan from a pesticide company. Come on!" she said, jumping up and pulling on her jacket, swaying slightly with a head rush.

"How will we get there?" asked Dan, getting to his feet a little more cautiously.

Lucy chucked him a cycle helmet. "How do you think?" Her hidden smile pushed the mask upwards at the sides of her face.

***

The two-mile cycle to Lucy's work was surreal. Visibility had improved since the morning, as the number of seeds floating in the wind had eased. But the soft, sepia carpet had become damp overnight, and slippery. Both Lucy and Dan nearly came off their bikes as they initially underestimated the treachery of the surface. The fluff was reducing to clumps, and the mustard shade turning translucent.

In their haste, neither of them had mentally prepared for the new rows of bodies they'd see lining each street they passed. The buses were emptier, too, presumably a combination of people staying home out of fear, or their occupants steadily dwindling in number as the disease spread. The most disturbing sight, however, was the collapsed body of a soldier; a crumpled heap of camouflage, his limbs twisted, wrists bent over, fingers sticking out at jarring angles. His tortured face was mostly concealed as it kissed the asphalt beneath his mask. Seeds had begun to land on his uniform, making it hard to judge how long he'd been there.

Lucy swallowed grimly, suppressing her vomit reflex, the acidic aftertaste lingering at the back of her mouth long after they passed the soldier's wilted body. That his uniform had meant nothing to the disease, that the people here to protect them were themselves just as vulnerable as she was … She shivered and pushed the pedals harder. Most disturbing was that his body hadn't been collected by his fellow soldiers. If the military couldn't survive this thing, then how were the two of them going to make it?

They arrived at her workplace, an otherwise deserted stretch of the city. With no residential population here, it was one of the few streets not adorned with corpses. The large glass doors to the lobby were locked shut, so Dan hurled a trash can at them several times. It created an almighty racket. Lucy's relief was immense when the glass finally gave way on the fourth attempt, leaving them free to tiptoe through the shards and inside. The intruder alarm stayed silent, neutered by the lack of electricity. Lucy gave a guilty glance at the empty concierge desk, mentally apologizing to the absent custodians for vandalizing their lobby.

They brought the bikes just inside the glass building and propped them up against the internal wall before heading up the main stairs, soon reaching Lucy's company's offices on the third floor. She instinctively tried her swipe card, which had no effect. Again, Dan smashed the door into the office, this time using a nearby fire extinguisher and succeeding in one deft blow. The glass crunched beneath their feet as they crossed into the otherwise silent space. Her deserted open-plan office stretched before them, filled with defunct Mac Pros, ergonomic desk chairs, and unwatered pot plants.

"This way," she said, leading down the central avenue towards a partitioned section at the end. Something in the periphery of her vision moved.

"What was that?" she said, spinning around to face the staff lounge.

"What was what?" said Dan, looking from Lucy to the lounge.

"I thought I saw … Nothing, it was just a rat. I saw its tail disappearing. It's fine, I'm not scared of them, I just wasn't expecting it. I guess it's found the food in the staff kitchen. Come on, this way," she said, continuing forwards.

"Looks like you've got a leak in the staff area – there's water on the floor," said Dan, catching up. "You should get it checked out when this place reopens."

The studio door opened without resistance, revealing an array of green screens, soft boxes, and cameras mounted on tripods, all entirely redundant without power.

"There they are!" exclaimed Lucy, spotting the props rack to the side of the room where three yellow-and-white hazmat suits hung in pristine condition. Their creased, shiny arms draped limply above the face shields, gloves, and black wellie boots piled below.

She and Dan quickly crossed over to the rack and immediately began kicking off their shoes.

"Wait," said Dan, who was about to plunge a leg into the suit he was holding, "do these go over our clothes or are they instead of them?"

Lucy tried to recall how they'd done everything in the advert. "I imagine they'll get pretty hot – they're basically all plastic. So maybe just underwear and a T-shirt?"

"OK: minimal base layer," agreed Dan. He dropped the suit and began wrestling his jeans off. Lucy hesitated for a moment, recalling the order of layers, then began doing the same.

The suit shell was essentially a plasticized onesie: a single garment from top to toe. Lucy pulled each leg on, then the arms, wriggling the top half over her shoulders and into place before pulling the front zipper up from her navel to her chin.

"Like this." She reached across and tucked Dan's zip beneath the Velcro safety flap on the collar. "Grab a mask and goggles," she said, pointing him to the three piles on the floor.

"Haven't they been used?" he hesitated.

"Only way before the outbreak. They're better quality than these, though, surely?" she said, tapping her existing mask. "You ready?" She picked up two of the specialist breathing filters and handed one to Dan.

"Ready," he confirmed.

They ripped off their cheap face masks and goggles, discarding them onto the floor by their shoes. Lucy wrestled the new face mask over her nose and mouth. It was thicker, and marginally harder to breathe through. The goggles, however, were a definite improvement; broader than a snorkelling mask, they significantly improved her field of vision compared to the narrow, misty swimming pair she'd set off with.

"All good?" asked Dan, adjusting his straps.

"I think so," said Lucy, still adapting to the new breathing filter. "Hoods next," she added, pulling hers on. The elasticated lip kept the hood snug against her forehead and cheeks, fully covering her hairline and ears.

She grabbed the long rubber gloves and pulled a pair on while Dan fussed over his hood positioning. They were as long as her forearm.

"You tape me in, then I'll do you," she said, passing him some silver duct tape.

He taped around both glove holes – just below the elbow – so that each glove was properly sealed to her suit. Lucy swiftly reciprocated, sealing Dan in.

They both affixed the hard-plastic visors, which shielded their faces from ear to ear, extending from forehead to below the chin. Lastly, they pulled on a pair of black wellies each, taping them to their suit legs.

"How d'ya like my new threads?" said Dan, strutting around her in a circle.

Lucy laughed. "You look ridiculous."

"What? I look sick! I look like a riot cop," he added with a proud nod, still strutting.

"You look like a beekeeper," she retorted. "How's your breathing?" she asked, noticing the slight mist her breath generated against the inside of her visor.

"Fine. Though these boots are a little small. What d'you wanna do about our clothes?" he replied, pointing to the discarded pile next to them.

Approaching voices made them both spin around.

"People!" hissed Lucy, her heart rate soaring.

The voices were close enough to be in the open-plan office now.

"Quickly!" urged Lucy, heading straight for the emergency exit on the far side of the studio. The voices got closer still, with shouts of "Hello?" echoing through the hallway.

Lucy kicked the emergency exit bar open. The door swung out onto the fire escape, hitting the railing behind with a clang and bouncing back. Catching the rebound with her hand, she leapt out onto the small platform, turning to check Dan was with her.

"Dan, quick!" she cried as the two figures burst into the studio.

Limping towards them at speed was her boss, Myles, with his petite blonde girlfriend glued to his elbow.

"Hey!" yelled Myles, leading the advance. His voice was muffled by a face mask, but his eyes were daggers and his fists were balled. "Stop right there! This is private prop–"

It wasn't clear whether he'd recognized them or not in the suits, but Lucy was willing to bet that at this stage it wouldn't make a difference – he needed the suits as much as they did.

"Go!" she cried, slamming the fire door shut. Dan threw himself at the rusty fire-escape ladder and Lucy followed. The cumbersome attire hampered their speed. Dan jumped the last few steps and landed on the steel platform below with a clatter, prompting Lucy to copy.

"Come on!" he shouted back, already starting down the next level. Lucy kept as close as possible without crushing his retreating hands underfoot. The studio fire exit crashed open again with a clang. Lucy scrambled down the steps as fast as she could, glancing up to see Myles stumbling out onto the platform above. He glared over the edge at them, and for a split second she thought she saw recognition in his eyes before he vanished. The clattering of rapid footsteps on the ladder above signalled the hunt was on, as he began to chase after them.

Lucy looked back down and concentrated on the descent; Dan had reached the last rungs of the bottom ladder and it was a big drop now. He hit the solid ground below with a thud, but managed to stay on both feet.

"Come on, Luce!" he yelled, gesturing for her to jump.

She looked up and saw Myles's hand sweep over the side of the platform two levels up as he raced to the next ladder. She cast her eyes downward again and jumped, Dan catching her as she stumbled forward. He grabbed her hand and they ran towards the front of the building.

"Look!" cried Lucy as they rounded the corner. "That's Myles's car!" she said, pointing at the stationary vehicle across the road. "It wasn't there before!"

"How the hell is he still driving?" cried Dan, gasping for breath as they charged back into the lobby.

"No idea – watch the glass!" shouted Lucy, as they darted over to their bikes and ripped them from the wall.

"Hey! Stop!" yelled a voice from above them in the lobby. Jennifer was at the top of the staircase, clutching the third hazmat suit. "I said stop!" she screamed, all timidity vanishing as she hurried down the stairs towards them.

Dan hurled both bikes outside, over the shards, and the pair scrambled after them.

"Let's go!" he yelled, snatching his bike from the ground and leaping onto it. Lucy didn't need telling twice. The pair took off fast, hurtling down the slippery sidewalk and onto the road.

Dan swerved to the side a little as he looked over his shoulder.

"OK, this is bad!" he cried, as she pulled level.

Lucy glanced backward; Myles had made it down the fire escape and now he and Jennifer were converging on the car.

"This way!" yelled Dan, pulling ahead again and swerving left. Myles's revving engine projected his fury down the street.

Dan hooked into a side street that was too narrow for cars. Lucy followed him, barely avoiding skidding off the bike as she took the corner at speed, pulling her front wheel up as they mounted the sidewalk. Wheelspin echoed around the otherwise silent district as Myles released his handbrake, hurtling down the slushy road towards them.

Lucy kept glancing backward as they sped down the alleyway, her hot, rapid breathing fogging up the visor. Myles's car raced past the turning they'd taken and out of sight, audibly skidding around the parallel block.

The light at the end of the alleyway grew closer as the pair peddled desperately, racing to emerge before Myles could cut them off.

A series of gunshots rang out from ahead, followed by the screech of car brakes under immense strain. A military truck sped past the backstreet opening, giving a fleeting glimpse of three uniformed soldiers, the last of whom was mounting the gun turret. Dan slammed on his brakes, Lucy did the same, and they came to a stop just yards from the opening. Not daring even to peer out of the alley,

Lucy looked at Dan and suddenly realized how conspicuous their outfits were.

"Myles could be telling the patrol we stole the suits!" she gasped.

"We've gotta turn back!" said Dan, struggling to regulate his volume in the panic.

Lucy spun her bike around, setting off the way they'd come, her legs screaming from oxygen debt. She pushed on, forcing the cranks around until she reached the original entrance to the passage again. Stopping, she peered out cautiously onto the street ahead: it was deserted.

"You lead," gasped Dan. "You know this area best."

***

More than an hour passed as they weaved through a patchwork of slippery, undulating backstreets, avoiding the main roads.

"Dan," said Lucy, halting atop a hilly road overlooking the water. "Look – the beach."

Covering the sand were piles of dead, washed-up marine life, all coated in glistening yellow liquid. The yellow waters were themselves now textured by a layer of fluffy golden seeds growing on top. The seeds drifted inland in their thousands as the wind scooped up the never-ending supply and spread it across the city.

"You hear that?" said Lucy, as a chopping sound approached.

A helicopter came into view. It was flying slowly, and trailing a rigid cable a few metres above the water surface.

"What *is* that?" she asked, squinting.

"It looks like they're dropping something onto the water – maybe a pesticide or something?" said Dan, peering out with his hand raised to his brow.

The helicopter began a vertical climb of several hundred feet, and retracted the cable. A bright light appeared on the open side of the helicopter as a flare was tossed downward, tumbling through the air.

The second it hit the water surface, the entire seafront erupted in flame. The helicopter took off out of sight as Lucy and Dan stared on in amazement. The flames, metres tall, engulfed the oily-yellow scum, cloaking the coastline in fire and thick black smoke.

"You reckon that's gonna work?" asked Lucy, as her eyes glazed over, mesmerized by the lapping flames.

"I reckon it's gonna wipe out the pier," said Dan, turning his bike around and pushing off.

***

As they continued their improvised route home, it became clear that the seafront wasn't the only place fire was being tactically deployed. Lucy and Dan watched as the military used a flamethrower to burn seeds that had been piled up in the middle of a residential street. A fire truck stood on duty, ready to intervene, while the surviving residents watched on fearfully from their doorsteps, many with wrapped bodies at their feet.

The hazmat suits made for sweaty work. Lucy and Dan's rate of pedalling had dropped significantly now that they were clear of Myles. Lucy was keen to keep her breathing rate low whenever possible, to avoid exacerbating the mask's resistance.

As they locked their bikes up at the side of their building later that afternoon, Lucy's eye was drawn to the paving. "What the ... Dan, is this stuff *growing*?"

"Don't get too close!" he warned, as Lucy knelt down to investigate.

Protruding through the mustard-coloured layer of spores was a sapling. It was wet, and its green-yellow leaves were covered in beads of moisture.

"That makes no sense," said Lucy, standing back up. "It's gotta be nearly five o'clock, and this area's been in the sun for the whole afternoon. Yet the ground's still wet, and this plant's wet. *No*," she corrected, quickly, "the ground's dry. It's the seeds that are wet."

"Maybe they retain moisture?" suggested Dan, who had remained standing up. "A lot of plants do."

"Not on the outside they don't," she countered. "Not in direct sunlight, and to this extent."

"Maybe it's not water, then?" considered Dan. "It could be something else – something that doesn't evaporate as easily?"

Voices sounded nearby. Dan immediately pressed himself flush against the wall and Lucy copied. Two neighbours from their building were carrying out a body. From the age gap they looked to be father and son, although the face masks made the relationship harder to judge. Neither man paid her or Dan the slightest bit of attention, too preoccupied as they were with the disposal of what was presumably a family member. The younger man, who looked around thirty, put a hand on the other man's shoulder, as the latter visibly shook with grief, surveying the body he'd laid out. The pair stood like that for a long minute before the son delicately led the father back into the building.

Dan held them in position for a further minute. Before they entered their building, they painstakingly wiped the soles of their hazmat suits onto the slimy entrance mat.

"We're gonna need to think of an alternative to this," noted Dan, looking at the sodden mat.

They repeated the immaculate wiping routine again on the eighth floor, checking each other's soles for seeds at least three times before they felt safe entering their home.

When they finally got into their apartment, the last of Lucy's adrenaline wore off. She slumped, sliding her back down the wooden door until she sat, legs splayed out on the floor before her. Her head pounded with thirst and hunger. Dan similarly succumbed to exhaustion and slumped adjacent to her.

"We can't do it like this," mumbled Lucy. "We need to drink. And eat. There's no point having these suits if we starve inside them. I think we need to risk taking them off for both."

"What we need," considered Dan, dozily, "is a canary."

"What?"

"Like miners used to have. They'd have a canary in the mine, which would die when the gas levels got dangerous. We need something like that in here. A pet – something that we can use to gauge if the air's safe to breathe or not. The disease kills everything, right? So if we've got, like, a budgie in here, and it's alive, then we can assume the air's safe."

"What if we take our suits off *then* the budgie dies?" countered Lucy. "Then it's too late to save ourselves."

"So we wait. Three hours – that's what the radio said."

"They said twenty-four," corrected Lucy.

"Yeah, but three if it's going to kill you. If we've got a canary and it's still alive three hours after we get back, then we'd know the air's safe, right?"

"What if our canary just so happens to have a natural resistance that we don't?" frowned Lucy.

"Then we're screwed," conceded Dan. "But we're also screwed if we don't drink or eat. So on balance –"

"It's worth the risk," completed Lucy. She nodded, looking around their partially sealed apartment. It made sense; without a vent and an airlock, they needed some other indication of the air's viability.

"Where are we going to get a canary from?" she asked, dreading the answer as she pictured them trying to break into a pet shop of different starving animals.

"The Spanish woman from downstairs," said Dan, renewed purpose in his voice. "I bet you she had a pet – a cat, or something."

"But she had the disease."

"She might have caught it when she was out. She had her key in her hand, right? So she was returning to the apartment, not leaving it. Maybe she's got a pet in there that's still alive?"

It was worth a try, for sure. Lucy hauled her fatigued body up from the ground as Dan marched off into the bedroom determinedly, returning with two flashlights.

Lucy retrieved the Spanish lady's bleached key from the sideboard where they'd left it the night before and steeled herself. "OK. Let's do it."

***

The door opened with a click. She checked Dan was still close by her shoulder then gently pushed it open. "Hello?" she called out, hoping desperately there'd be no reply. Lucy took a few steps into the deserted apartment, and as she did so began to notice details of the dead woman's life.

The windows were covered by thin white embroidered curtains – the sort of ornate patterns that were all the rage a century ago. Hanging on the walls were a number of religious artefacts: crucifixes, pictures of the Virgin Mary, and figurines of assorted saints. In the corner, next to the TV, was a small prayer stool with a gospel resting on the shelf. Manuela had clearly been a devout woman.

On the kitchen worktop were two packets of medication.

"Take two tablets daily, orally, with water," said Lucy, reading one of the labels aloud.

"Are you paying attention?" snapped Dan. "We're on a mission here."

She mentally swore at him, but didn't pick a fight, knowing that he had a point. She placed the tablets back down and explored the apartment further. The woman's bedroom was almost completely pitch black; the curtains were fully drawn and the lights were out. Standing on the threshold and peering in, Lucy cast her flashlight around the room.

She jumped and backed up a few paces as a scuffling noise from the dark corner startled her.

"Bullseye!" cheered Dan, appearing by her side and shining his light onto the terrified-looking hamster. "I knew she'd have a pet," he chimed triumphantly, walking towards the cage and swearing loudly as he marched his shin into the side of the bed.

"I'll get it, you point the lights," said Lucy, handing him her flashlight and taking over as Dan nursed his shin.

Lucy moved the hamster cage into the middle of the main room and they hunted for the woman's stash of pet food; the pathetic ball of fur looked as hungry as they were, and they needed it to not die.

"What kind of a grown woman keeps a pet hamster, anyway?" asked Dan, as they rifled through Manuela's cupboards. "I take it back," he said immediately. "She's got Twinkie bars. She's a saint. Rest in peace Manuela, bringer of Twinkies."

"Knock it off, Dan," grumbled Lucy. "You should respect the dead – *especially* in their own home. Now let's go," she said, standing up with the cage in one hand and an armful of pet food in the other. "We can always come back if we need more."

"Fine," said Dan, stuffing Twinkie bars into a box of cereal he'd also decided to appropriate. "Make sure we stick it by the front door, yeah? We wanna be able to see him when we get in. Oh, and shotgun choosing the name. I name you –" He paused, while Lucy walked towards the door with scathing indifference. "– Madonna, the Virgin Hamster. Presumably, I don't know. Maybe this guy got laid a lot in high school. Or girl. I really don't know much about hamsters."

Lucy pressed on without responding, carrying Madonna the Virgin Hamster up the stairs, with Twinkie cereal boy in tow. She stepped back and let Dan open the door. "Welcome to your new home, Madonna," she said, crossing the threshold. "Please don't be infected."

SEVEN

Canaries

The end-of-curfew siren woke Lucy with a jolt. Unlike the three blasts used to begin the curfew at night, the morning signal was just one blast of around eight seconds. It was an appalling way to wake up.

Dan, however, didn't stir, the lucky git. She instinctively went to rub her eyes, banging her glove-covered hands straight into her visor. She groaned, flopping back down onto the mattress where she lay, listening to the crinkling of her suit. An amplified army announcement from the street interrupted her wallowing.

She turned towards the source of the sound, her hazmat suit creaking and crumpling as it twisted beneath her. The truck slowly rumbled by, repeating the same message that KGO 810 had broadcast two nights previously: "All able-bodied citizens: report to City Hall for immediate reassignment. Rations will no longer be delivered. You must collect them in person. Report to City Hall."

Her eyes fell upon a picture on her bedside table – a framed portrait she'd sketched of the two of them, illuminated as it was by the morning light. She turned again and looked at her sleeping partner now, noting their matching plastic pyjamas. Perhaps she should do them a fresh portrait.

She gave Dan a nudge, then a slightly less tender one which actually woke him up. "We need to go."

Madonna was still alive when they awoke, so once again they took the calculated risk to remove their hazmat suits. Seizing the precious window of safety, they hastily ate, cleaned themselves using wet wipes, and defecated, before putting the suits straight back on. The suits were off and on again within twelve minutes (Dan timed them using the wall clock). The volume of food they had to gobble down left them both feeling physically ill afterwards, but it was necessary given that they didn't know when, or where, it would next be safe to eat.

Once again they called on Manuela's apartment for help. They needed to be out of the suits to be able to take a shit, which meant the hamster-certified air of their apartment was the only safe place to risk doing it. But they'd sealed up all the utilities, and an ever-mounting pile of sewage in the apartment's stagnant toilet didn't seem like a desirable plan. The inglorious resolution they settled on involved Dan's bucket, a makeshift lid, and a shameful hurried journey downstairs wearing the hazmat suits to Manuela's apartment, where they emptied the bucket into her disused toilet.

"We need to remember to flush that toilet when the power comes on next," noted Dan, returning the bucket to their apartment before the pair of them set off out.

With calories at a premium now, they decided they should get the bus to City Hall. But thirty minutes elapsed and no bus came. Lucy had never felt so grateful for bus-shelter seats. The number of people waiting grew from three to twenty. Each new arrival eyed her and Dan up with deep suspicion, glaring at the fully suited couple from beneath their simple face masks and giving them a wide berth.

"Where'd you get those suits?" challenged a new arrival, staggering over to them. He was in his forties, unshaven, and drinking openly from a bottle of Scotch.

Lucy looked away, blushing.

"Hey! I'm talking to you!" he said, getting closer still. She felt the eyes of all twenty other commuters staring at her.

"Sir, you should be wearing a mask," replied Dan.

"Masks are for pussies," laughed the man, taking a swig from his bottle. "And those fucking things," he continued, gesturing to their hazmat suits with derision, "are for faggots."

Lucy looked at Dan, nervously, as the drunkard opened his arms wide, inviting retaliation.

Dan simply stared at him, blinking freely, not giving anything away.

"Yeah? What you gonna do about it?" said the man, swaying. "What you gonna do, Mr. Suit Man?"

Dan continued to look at the man, calmly.

"Fucking whatever," spluttered the drunkard, dropping his hands back to his sides in disappointment. "Fucking suit people," he mumbled, swearing at them and everyone else at the bus stop for good measure before staggering away, muttering to himself.

Lucy exhaled heavily and looked to Dan, whose expression had hardened.

"You OK?" she asked.

"Fine," replied Dan, clenching and unclenching his fist. "He was just a bum. Not worth engaging with. Wouldn't have done us much good if I'd laid him out on the sidewalk. He's probably gonna be dead soon enough anyway, wandering around like that without a mask."

"Unless he's naturally resistant," noted Lucy, "in which case god help us if we've got to rebuild mankind off of his shoulders."

A police patrol slowed as it drew parallel with the bus stop. "This route is out of use, people," said the officer, speaking through the bullhorn. "There's still a bus route working over on Masonic Avenue, it'll get you to City Hall," she said, surveying the crowd.

Lucy shuffled her feet beneath the seat. It felt like the cop was staring at her and Dan. Did she know they were behind the office break-in yesterday? How would they possibly explain the stolen hazmat suits? What was their cover story?

The officer pulled away without further comment, and the tension gripping Lucy's chest eased. She and Dan joined the trail of people now steadily making their way to Masonic Avenue.

The number of seeds drifting in the air had reduced again. Occasional yellow specks danced in the breeze, but it was a far cry from the blizzard they'd experienced before.

The number of bodies, however, continued to grow. Dozens more victims lined the sidewalk, their corpses pressing into the translucent layer of gloop that was replacing the fluffy mustard-yellow spores.

The bus-seekers quickly defaulted to walking on the road, to avoid passing the bodies littering the sidewalk. Lucy held back deliberately so that she and Dan could walk behind the crowd. She hadn't anticipated how alienating their protective layer would be.

The wet spores made a loud patting sound underfoot, like walking through a shallow puddle.

While the streets avoided the problem of human bodies, they were dotted with the carcasses of small animals – mainly cats and rodents – which were seemingly being marinated in the slush.

The people ahead slowed to a stop as they reached a corner, which they began to bunch around. The sound of barking carried over, prompting Lucy and Dan to move to the edge of the group, where they could peer around the corner to see what was happening.

A dog stood in the middle of the street ahead, barking incessantly, and scarpering from one side to the other. Occasionally it stopped and pawed furiously at its head, then barked at the ground before jumping away and circling back on itself, or weaving across to another patch.

"It looks rabid," said Lucy. "We need to keep the hell away from it."

"I think these guys might be able to help," said Dan, spotting a military patrol advancing down the street.

The dog turned towards the engine noise and increased its incessant barking, interspersing it with deep growls.

The patrol slowed until it was a few yards from the feral animal, then turned side-on. The passenger soldier drew his handgun and took aim at the growling dog, firing two shots directly into its body.

The dog crumpled with a yelp and lay twitching on the ground. The patrol drove on immediately.

Nervously, the group edged forwards, the other civilians talking among themselves as they pressed on, giving the dead animal a wide berth.

"Luce, what are you doing?" asked Dan, as she broke away from the group and knelt down close to the motionless dog. There were clumps of fur missing from its grimy, matted coat.

"I don't recognize this breed," she said, standing up and circling it slowly. "There's something different about it."

"Yeah, it was foaming at the mouth and ready to rip our legs off," said Dan, impatiently. "We need to get a move on, Luce. I don't wanna miss the only bus to City Hall and end up waking all the way there."

He began setting off after the other walkers.

"It won't be the *only* bus," she said, catching up.

SPLAT.

"Fuck!" cried Dan, jumping to the side in disgust.

"Wow," said Lucy, looking up to see if more were coming. Blue skies; nothing overhead but the occasional cloud and some lilting seeds. "That's certainly a first," she said, turning her attention back downward to the smashed-up bird by Dan's feet. Its glistening white feathers were ruffled, sticking out at odd angles in line with the splayed posture. Its black eye stared straight up at the sky. Lucy crouched down and looked closely at the unfortunate creature. Large droplets of moisture clung to its entire body.

"Luce, the bus!" said Dan, pointing to the crowd of people who had begun to jog towards something around the next corner. Abandoning the bird, the pair of them ran after the group.

They caught up just in time, as the last person was boarding. It was standing room only for the entire twenty-minute journey. Lucy's ears pricked at the slightest throat-clearing, turning each instance into the thundering death coughs of her deceased neighbour. She stared at the other passengers through her hazmat suit. They looked so vulnerable in their jeans and hoodies. Were those face masks really going to keep them all alive? She felt like an observer in a laboratory, watching the busload of test subjects from behind a safety screen. A nearby passenger sneezed twice, making Lucy shudder.

Such a high concentration of people flew in the face of basic disease control. But with no cars running, it was the only way to get people to City Hall, and they needed workers to get power back online. Without power, there was no hope of modern medicine or sanitation being restored, and those things were key to the survival of the population in the face of this new disease. Or at least, that's what Lucy assumed was behind City Hall's logic.

The bus pulled into the City Hall complex where tens of thousands of people stood outside in long, snaking numbered lines. Each line filtered through a different part of the building's complex, and out of sight, so Lucy had no way of telling how long each one really was. But if the people outside were anything to go by, there could easily be a hundred thousand civilians gathered in total, if not more.

There was a heavy military presence; troops patrolled the lines, swiftly quelling any dissenters and dumping troublemakers to the back of the lines. Other soldiers patrolled the top of the City Hall building, scrutinizing the crowds.

Before anyone could exit the bus, a sergeant stepped aboard, holding a megaphone up to his mask.

"Listen up. There are five lines outside. You will go and stand in the line that best fits your skill set. At the end of that line you will be assigned your new place of work. At the end of your shift you will be entitled to collect your rations."

"Wait, so they're only giving out regular rations in exchange for work now?" said Lucy. But before Dan could reply, the sergeant continued.

"There are a *lot* of people here, so be prepared to queue for some time. Now I will only say this once, so pay attention. Line one is for military, line two is for medics, line three is for engineers, line four is agriculture, and line five is anyone else."

With that, he disappeared off the bus and into the crowd.

The passengers spilled out onto the forecourt and began trickling into different lines.

"Where should we go?" asked Lucy, as people jostled them off the bus. "You're obviously in the military line."

"And you're obviously agriculture," said Dan.

"Right," said Lucy, "but I don't want us to be separated again."

"Me neither," agreed Dan, casting his eyes around. "We'll have to lie. Just say we've got no relevant skills. We'll go line five. I'm not leaving you this time."

She took his gloved hand in hers and they made their way over to the back of the colossal line, as dozens more people joined with them. Five was predictably the most heavily subscribed queue, with the longest wait time. Tens of thousands of people stood before them, soldiers patrolling as scores of new arrivals flooded in by the busload. A few people who appeared to show symptoms were swiftly removed from the line and taken out of sight.

It was almost four hours before Dan and Lucy's turn came. Only once they'd finally made it inside the City Hall building could Lucy see how the line ended. A large function room contained twenty desks where individuals were processed. At each desk sat a military officer and a clerk, both of whom, to Dan and Lucy's surprise, wore hazmat suits.

"Stall E!" barked the flustered soldier overseeing line five's flow, pointing Lucy and Dan to a vacant stall.

The officer behind the desk of stall E was a diminutive, bespectacled man, with a crown of grey hair resting on his scalp, and an expression of extreme stress on his face, all just about visible from behind his plastic visor. His expression appeared to ease a little when Lucy and Dan arrived, seemingly recognizing kindred hazmat spirits, or at least people less likely to infect him than the others waiting. Not that it made his tone any less severe.

"You afraid of heights?" he enquired, looking at Dan first.

"Not especially," replied Dan.

"Good. You're assigned to pylons. Take this form and see that guy over there," he said, gesturing minimally to a secondary booth ahead.

"We're sticking together," said Dan, gesturing to Lucy.

"Then why the hell didn't you say so in the first place? Goddamnit!" whined the officer, snatching the form back from Dan's hand. "Both of you, head over there," he said, scribbling something on two forms and pointing to a stall labelled *Assignment*. "Next!" he bellowed, as his guard assistant shoved the two of them along. The guard's gun and hazmat combination made him look like a low-budget film extra.

They got to the next stall and handed the papers over. This officer only had a mask on, but seemed much better disposed than his colleague. "Looks like you guys have hit the big time," he said, deadpan. "Garbage duty. Grab your ration bags now and report to the East section. Find a truck and hop aboard. Got it?"

They headed sideways to the ration line where they were issued with their rations. One of the perks of garbage duty, it turned out, was that they got their rations upfront – but only because they wouldn't be finishing their daily shifts at the City Hall like the other workers.

After once again refusing to be separated, Lucy and Dan both got assigned to the same truck where they were dispatched on their first shift immediately – at one p.m., according to the on-board clock.

As they rode up front in the garbage truck, the scale of the devastation became clear; street after street was awash with bodies. Only then did it dawn on Lucy: it was their job to collect them.

***

By the end of the day they had almost become completely anaesthetized to the expressions of pain and anguish on the bodies they swung into the back of the truck. Early on they'd been forced to abandon attempts to handle the bodies with care; the scale and difficulty of the task demanded pragmatism alone.

Neither she nor Dan spoke much all day, numbed by the grim repetition. Their driver didn't utter a word during the entire shift either, making no attempt to invest in his new colleagues.

Within a single afternoon they had collected hundreds of bodies, but covered less than two square miles of the city. Adults, children, animals; everything went in the truck to be incinerated the same evening.

Lucy, confronted by the faces of young children, sometimes still in the arms of their dead parents, nearly threw up on several occasions. The closed, unblemished storefronts of Starbucks and Urban Outfitters looked like museum pieces frozen in time, framed in the eerie cold light of the dust cloud. Silently, achingly, Lucy and Dan systematically removed all trace of the dystopian scene that had unfolded around them.

But nothing could have prepared Lucy for when they found Cassie. Her body was like all the others, paralyzed in a state of writhing agony, her face distorted by the pain that dominated every muscle upon it, her eyes pallid and sorrowful, the burst capillaries now faded. She must've died a day or two ago. What hurt the most was that no one had covered her body. Had she died alone? Or had the people she'd been with died too? Maybe they'd already put their bodies in the truck.

Lucy didn't cry, she just stood, in shock, and stared at her best friend's lifeless body where it lay, abandoned in the street, terminated by whatever it was that was decimating mankind. She had deserved more than this.

"Come on," said Dan gently, moving to stand over Cassie's shoulders, the heavier part of the body. "We'll do it together," he said, somehow managing to sound compassionate in the face of what they were about to do. They'd quickly learned with all the other bodies – apart from the smaller pets and the babies, which could be done with a single arm – that it required two people; one on each end, to swing the body backward then release, to propel it forward over the lip of the truck and into the growing pile inside. Occasionally this was followed by the sickening crunching of bones as the machine necessarily compacted its load, to make space for the next batch. But Cassie landed quietly, and out of sight.

***

They were given a light chlorine rinse in their suits back at the depot before being dismissed for the day. It turned out City Hall didn't want its new undertakers to die on the job.

When they got home, Madonna greeted them with small squeaks for food, shielded from the horrors that lay outside her caged sanctuary. Neither knew what to say, both completely hollowed out by the ordeal. Dan switched on his phone and set a timer for three hours, during which they both collapsed onto the bed and slept in their suits.

The alarm woke Lucy, and she woke Dan. Knowing the air was safe, they silently undressed and washed themselves down with wipes before putting on regular clothes. To Lucy it felt like cheating. Make-believe.

The fact of the day stood as a wall between the two of them. They remained physically exhausted, and neither had the stomach for food, but they force-fed themselves. Lucy knew their ongoing survival depended on them replenishing calories when they were available. The new ration bag sat open on the kitchen table and she stared at it, bitterly resenting how it had come to be in their possession.

"We're keeping other people alive," said Dan, breaking the silence. "By doing this, I mean." He nodded to himself several times, as if repeating the sentiment internally like a mantra. But his eyes fell downward and his head soon came to a stop.

Lucy stretched out her arms, clenching her jaw and gripping either side of the table as if it were spinning out of control.

Dan got up, moving over and carefully taking her in his arms. "I'm so sorry about Cassie," he said, quietly. Lucy nodded, staring at the table, her eyes unfocused.

His skin warmed hers. It was the first time they'd had proper contact in days. He anchored her, arms wrapped around her chest, face nestled into her shoulder, his breathing making a small patch of the back of her top warm and damp. All of these senses she registered as comforting and yet she felt nothing. Cassie was gone.

A knock at the door broke the long embrace; they both jumped, startled, exchanging worried looks as they returned to the real world. Dan reached for a baseball bat and slowly made his way to the door, while Lucy kept her distance in case he needed to take a swing with it.

"Wait!" cried Lucy as Dan reached for the lock. "Here!"

She handed him his face mask, and pulled her own over her mouth.

He peered through the marble then turned to her and nodded before opening first the chain lock and then the main lock, swinging the front door open to reveal a soldier.

"Daniel Jeffries?" enquired the private through his protective mask.

"Yes?" replied Dan, nervously.

"This is for you," announced the soldier, producing an envelope and handing it to Dan before turning on his heels and retreating down the stairs.

Dan closed the door and relocked it. He turned the item in his hands as he rejoined Lucy at the table.

"What is it?" asked Lucy, noting the concern on his face.

"I don't know. Must be something to do with Dad," he said, tapping the government emblem. He tore the envelope open and laid the letter out on the table.

URGENT AND CONFIDENTIAL read the subject line. Below that, a subtitle read: *Reference: Adrian Jeffries, White House Chief of Staff.*

The letter had taken several days to reach them, going by the date printed across it, and the body copy had clearly been sent out to multiple people – it wasn't a personalized message. Dan began to read, a small gap opening between his pursed lips as he continued, immediately lifting the letter back up off the table and bringing it closer to his eyes as they tracked rapidly from side to side. Lucy came around to his side so she could better read over his shoulder.

Dear Daniel,

You and your partner have been identified as persons of national importance, and vital to the reconstruction of America in the wake of the ongoing natural disaster. You and your partner have been designated a place on the evacuation train that will be departing from San Francisco to Washington DC in the next seven days. We have evidence to suggest that the airborne pathogen will begin to die out in a matter of days. Once that has been confirmed, the evacuation signal will sound across your city's curfew siren. It will sound five consecutive times instead of three. This will happen once only. Only designated evacuees such as yourselves will know what it means. When you hear this, you must immediately proceed to your mustering point, which is: Ashurst High School.

Bring no more than one suitcase or equivalent each, and rations for the four-day journey. You must be ready to evacuate at any time from this moment onwards.

Once in DC you will be transferred to the White House, where you will help coordinate our national response to the crisis. Should you fail to arrive for departure within three hours of the signal, you will be assumed dead, and the train will depart without you. You must bring ID and this letter to your mustering point. Do not tell anyone where you are going. Uninvited persons attending mustering stations may be shot.

Sincerely,

Alison Walcock, acting Secretary of State.

Beneath the typed message was a short handwritten note:

My son, I hope you're alive. I'll wait for you both in DC. Be on the train, worse is coming. Your sister is dead. So sorry to tell you like this. I love you. Dad.

Dan dropped the note and slumped against the wall, the letter falling from his hands onto the floor.

"Oh my god, Dan," said Lucy, rushing to her broken partner, drawing him up in her arms and pressing his head into her body as tightly as she could. Dan said nothing and just sat, his arms hanging by his sides, the words knocked from his body.

She held him for a long time, then slowly led him to bed, where she eased him into his face mask and goggles, and lay him down to sleep. Comatose from grief and shock, he didn't utter a word the whole time, but allowed himself to be moved.

Lucy held him and stroked his hair until he fell asleep, or at least closed his eyes to be alone. Drying her own eyes, she quietly began to pack their bags for the evacuation.

***

Lucy awoke with a start as the regular end-of-curfew siren sounded. She sat bolt upright and listened for more pulses but none came. Five iterations were what they were waiting for; they'd only have minutes to react and get moving. But as the silence stretched out, her heart rate normalized again. It was a useful realization, though – what would they do if the signal came while they were at work? The only option, if they were truly to be ready at any time, was to keep their luggage with them wherever they went now.

The image of Cassie's twisted body flashed vividly across Lucy's mind. She shut her eyes and shook her head in denial, reopening them to find her vision blurred behind a sheen of tears.

She walked over to the hamster cage. Carefully, she opened the ceiling gate and lifted the quivering Madonna out. The creature's racing heartbeat vibrated through her hand. She stroked its soft fur, marvelling at the simplicity of Madonna's world while tears streamed down her face. She could crush that innocent, beautiful thing in an instant, she thought.

Dan stirred from within the bedroom. Lucy lowered Madonna back into her cage, refastened the ceiling gate, and drained the tears from her goggles before he emerged.

Dan said few words over breakfast, visibly still reeling from the loss of his sister. He nearly left the house without putting his hazmat suit on, such was his preoccupation.

As they descended the stairs, clad in semi-breathable plastic and weighed down by huge hiking backpacks, Dan stopped at the fourth floor.

"Does this look right to you?" he asked, quietly, as Lucy pulled level.

The door to apartment 403 stood wide open, and a flickering light reflected off the walls.

"Who even lives here?" replied Lucy, peering around.

"We should check it out," said Dan, as Lucy knew he would. "That flickering looks like a candle. I don't want our whole building going up in flames if it's unattended."

He knocked and called out but no one answered. Cautiously, they entered the darkened homestead.

It was different in layout to theirs: smaller, with an open-plan kitchen-living area that defined the space. The blinds were drawn, blocking the outside world. The flickering light drew Lucy's eye to an interior door on the left, which also stood ajar. She beckoned to Dan, and the two of them moved closer.

"Hello?" she called out, hoping for a reply.

Dan reached out and grabbed Lucy's arm, stopping her in her tracks. He stepped forwards so that she was behind him, shielded. Leading the way, he delicately nudged the door open. It swung back without resistance. They edged forwards into the threshold.

On the far side of the room stood a single candle nestled within a large glass vase. It was almost burned out entirely. The candle gave a soft warmth to the well-furnished room, its irregular light quietly lapping at the two motionless bodies on the bed.

The elderly couple lay entwined in each other's arms. Adjacent to them, on the bedside table, stood an empty bottle of sleeping pills. The pair might have looked peaceful were it not for their torn flesh. Lucy recognized the incisions; she was no stranger to the work of rats.

Dan took off his backpack and leaned it against the wall. Throwing open the bedroom window, he peered down onto the street below.

"Let's get this done," he said, signalling to Lucy to grab the dead man's legs. "What? They're going in a garbage truck later, anyway."

"Who lit the candle?" asked Lucy, stalling. "It can't have burned all this time; they must have died days ago. You think someone's already found them?"

"Yeah, probably, and because they lit a candle instead of getting rid of the bodies, we've got to do it – before the whole building becomes a magnet for other problems. Now come on."

He stuck a hand under each of the old man's armpits, raising the torso off the mattress. Lucy winced as a loose flap of skin fell forward and dangled from the elderly face, revealing the muscle, bone, and tendons beneath. The hazmat suit sanitized the air but couldn't stop her brain from replicating the smell of rotting flesh. The sickening smell cloyed at her palate.

She took hold of the old man's legs, the wrinkles and elasticity of his skin detectable even through her thick suit gloves. Together they heaved his body to the window, balancing him on the sill before tipping him off. He fell quickly and landed on the street below with a thud, spraying the pavement with congealed blood. His wife followed.

"Fine," said Dan, dispassionately, as they exited the old couple's flat and closed the door behind them. "Time for work."

***

When they returned home that evening, Madonna was dead.

The caged hamster lay on its back, limbs contorted, its neck outstretched to the right as if trying to escape the rest of its diseased body. They stood in the hallway of their apartment, backpacks pressing the plastic hazmat suits into their sweaty backs, staring at the dead rodent. The disease had reached their home.

Stepping back out into the stairwell, Lucy closed the apartment door. She and Dan considered their next move. Staying in their infected apartment – in their hazmat suits – posed an unnecessary risk. On the balance of probabilities it made more sense to try somewhere else which may, on the off chance, be sanitary.

After some deliberation they identified only two practical options: 403 – the old couple's apartment, where the occupants had died from sleeping pills – or Manuela's place, where they'd found Madonna alive and well. The reality was that both environments had since been compromised by airflow, but Lucy and Dan were in agreement: moving presented the least threat.

They decided in favour of Manuela's apartment and put phase one into action. Lucy retrieved the key from their sideboard while Dan disposed of the hamster. He tore off the useless plastic seal they'd constructed around the kitchen window and slung Madonna's body out into the toxic night air, cursing as he slammed the window shut again. Next to him, Lucy tugged the plastic off the balcony doors and

129

looked out into the twilight. The seeds had disappeared from the wind, and their slushy remains had largely drained away from the sidewalks and roads. But still the disease lingered.

They retreated downstairs to Manuela's empty apartment. As Lucy clicked the lock open, she ducked as a startled pigeon flew wildly around the room, flapping frantically until it flew straight into the window and stunned itself.

"Grab the hamster cage!" yelled Lucy as she pounced on the bird, tenderly picking it up, securing it between her gloves.

Dan disappeared from the room, returning a minute later with the empty cage. He lifted the metal mesh up and Lucy placed the dozy bird inside, Dan quickly locking the frame again before it could escape.

"Looks like we've found our new canary," said Lucy, watching as the drowsy bird began dragging itself into an upright position.

"Technically it's a pigeon," replied Dan, grinning. "No wonder you dropped out of veterinary college."

Lucy gave him a spectacularly sarcastic smile through her mask and led the way back to their apartment, carrying their new ward.

***

The power hadn't come on in several days, and from their day job she and Dan knew why: the workforce was dying out quicker than it could be replaced. "System knowledge is dying with them," Dan surmised that night in bed. "We're going to have to start thinking longer term."

The death of Elvis the pigeon further complicated matters. Elvis succumbed after just two nights, his crumpled form signalling the danger within Manuela's apartment. His demise renewed their conviction that sleeping in the hazmat suits was critical, while forcing them to move to apartment 403.

"This is keeping us alive," Lucy reassured herself the morning after Elvis's passing, as she carried a bucket of her own excrement down the stairwell and outside the building. Now that their former dumping ground – Manuela's apartment – was contaminated, an alternative arrangement had become necessary. Lucy reached the bushes by the bike lock-up area and dug a small hole. She tipped the waste in then covered it over, unperturbed by the incredulous expression of a passer-by across the street – instead relieved to see another survivor around. The sapling she'd seen when they'd first stolen the suits had disappeared without a trace, along with the translucent-mustard gloop.

She replaced the bucket in 403 and agreed to wait for Dan while he quickly hunted for batteries upstairs in their actual apartment.

He returned breathless and pale.

"We've been robbed," he panted from the threshold.

Lucy hastened after him back up the stairs. The door of their home was wide open, the wooden frame splintered and smashed where the lock had been forced open.

"They took the food," said Dan, leading the way inside.

Lucy followed, registering the faint footprints on their polished wooden floor. One set was much smaller than the other.

"Check this," said Dan, passing her a note. "I mean, what the actual fuck, right?"

SORRY

"They left this?" said Lucy, reading the one-word message.

"On the kitchen table," nodded Dan. "The *audacity*! Robbing someone then leaving an apology note? Maybe they're just straight up mocking us?"

Lucy studied the message again: large block capitals, written with a red sharpie, on lined notepaper.

"At least they didn't get the antibiotics," said Lucy, glancing towards the bathroom. "I packed them – in our evac bags."

"*Bastards!*" he cried, thumping the wall. "We obviously can't ever stay here again – not with the door like that, and not when we're on someone's goddamned map!"

Lucy did a sweep through the apartment. The kitchen was a mess of open drawers and cupboard doors, but the bedroom and living room were exactly as they'd left them.

"Did they take anything else?" she asked, rejoining Dan in the corridor.

"I don't think so," replied Dan. "Think they just grabbed the food and left."

"Thank god we weren't sleeping here when they broke in."

"They might've robbed us in daytime, we can't be sure," he grumbled, kicking his boots against the skirting board.

"Think positive. Thanks to you we've still got half of our rations," said Lucy, rubbing his back. "We'll work through what we've got in 403, and when we're done, we'll get the rest from Manuela's."

"And then?" he challenged.

"Don't be like that," replied Lucy.

"Like what?"

"We got robbed, Dan, not shot. Get over your pride and stop taking this as some kinda personal failure – we don't have the energy for that."

Dan said nothing and stepped outside, leaving Lucy room to exit too before he pulled the broken door shut behind her, wedging it against the splintered frame.

"What's that?" she said, eyeing up the crowbar in his hand.

"Protection," he replied.

"You're bringing it to work?"

"What? No! I'm leaving it downstairs – in case anyone does try to rob us in the night."

As they retrieved their backpacks from 403 a noise, something between a long moan and a whine, pricked Lucy's ears.

"You hear that?" she asked Dan, pausing his rustling. "I think it's coming from the elevator – sounds like something's trapped in there."

Dan joined her by the doorway and listened. "Sounds like a cat."

"Yeah – which means the owner's probably trapped there too. We need to check it out."

Dan groaned, dropping his backpack again and fetching the crowbar. "This is *exactly* why I'm not a cat person."

They followed the wails downstairs to the third floor.

"Here!" said Lucy, training her head lamp on the elevator doors.

"I wish I'd never bought this stupid thing," complained Dan, wedging the crowbar between the elevator doors and leaning into it heavily.

"Watch out!" cried Lucy.

As Dan prised the elevator doors apart, water spilled out through the inch-wide gap, splashing out onto the hallway and down into the elevator shaft below.

"What the hell?" gasped Dan, stumbling backward and shaking the water off his suit.

The gushing stream quickly subsided to dripping. Lucy peered through the slit, her light illuminating the dark void beneath the elevator base, which was suspended around five feet above the floor – stuck between levels.

"Gimme a hand," said Dan, dropping the crowbar and placing his fingers along one of the door edges. Lucy copied, lining up against the opposite one. "Careful you don't fall inward. Alright, heave!"

As they each pulled a door back, a mangy cat darted from the elevator with a cry, landing on the floor and immediately springing down the dark stairwell out of sight.

"There's your cat," said Dan.

"I think we found the owner, too," said Lucy, looking upwards.

As they both stepped backwards, their beams illuminated the pile of rotting flesh and crumpled clothes on the dripping elevator floor.

"Flies. Gross," said Dan, switching off his head lamp. "What? I don't want them flying at me – you should turn yours off too."

Lucy frowned but covered her light, dimming it substantially. She could only see glimpses of the shiny, golden-shelled flies, which quickly dispersed.

"Come on," said Dan. "Let's get the bags and go. We've got work to do – and rations to earn."

***

134

"Whaddup! You guys must be my new colleagues!" cheered an unfamiliar garbage-truck driver as he pulled up that morning, throwing the passenger door open.

An upshot of working garbage duty was that they didn't have to ride the buses to City Hall anymore; they could walk a few blocks to the truck's route and get collected.

"They said you'd look weird – you guys look super weird!" yelled the driver from behind his face mask. "Get on up here now, don't be shy!" He beckoned them up and slid back over to the steering seat.

"The other guy died by the way, sorry about that, thought you should know. I'm Marco, who are you?"

And that was the beginning of the questions. Marco never really seemed to engage with any of their answers – and Dan never really engaged with Marco, preferring to let Lucy shoulder the brunt of the conversation. Not that she had to do much talking. Marco was like da Vinci's machine of perpetual small talk, happily filling all silence with never-ending observations and banalities – interspersed with very out-of-tune rock karaoke as he incessantly looped AC/DC live albums.

Reticent as Dan was, the driver's humour lifted both of their spirits a little during the long, arduous shifts. Unlike his predecessor, Marco didn't view their hazmat suits as a reason not to talk to them both. Rather, he found them a regular source of amusement and good fodder for his irrepressible chatter.

"You guys are so funny looking!" he would say every day, several times, before laughing happily. He'd then invariably be distracted by another ransacked burger joint that he used to love or – often – the outfits of the dead people they were about to collect. "Check out that guy's shoes – who even *wears* those, man!"

Marco's profoundly cheerful detachment from (or denial of) reality served them all well, but Lucy found herself studying him while listening. All of his conversation was in the present tense, and consisted of light-hearted tip-offs about where to get the best salami in town, or his buddy's tapas bar on Eighth. He spoke as if none of it had changed, and never once referred to the fact that they were stopping to collect human bodies instead of trash.

Lucy suspected he wasn't entirely sober. Fortunately the streets were devoid of other traffic or pedestrians, meaning it was just she and Dan who had to hope for the best as passengers.

The chatty reaper was also a well-connected man in the new world, it turned out, and was able to procure two living gerbils for Dan and Lucy in exchange for some of their rations.

Meanwhile the number of bodies was increasing faster than they could remove them. It meant they were stoking the incinerator with plenty of fuel each day, but presumably the power generated was being routed directly to hospitals and prisons – or at least, that's what Lucy assumed. She didn't know because they hadn't been able to tune into KGO 810 for over a week, and her military 'sources' had been replaced by the chatty AC/DC gerbil man. Maybe they weren't generating power at all, she considered, as the days passed; maybe they were just burning bodies.

"Eugh!" cried Lucy, leaping back and dropping her end of a corpse one afternoon.

"What the hell, Luce!" said Dan, still holding the heavy torso end.

"The body," said Lucy, staring at the corpse. "I felt the legs move!"

"Move?" said Dan, dropping the torso and stepping back.

"Not *move*, but … slip. I … Look!" she said, carefully sliding the dead man's trouser leg upward.

"What the …" said Dan, crouching for a closer look.

The leg had disintegrated to a hideous sloppy form.

"How long's this one been here? What is that, gangrene?" asked Dan.

"I'm not sure," said Lucy, pulling the trouser further up. "It's some kind of infection. Eugh, tapeworms! Boy has this one turned. Let's get it in the truck before I barf," said Lucy, bending down and clasping the hems of each trouser leg.

"On three," said Dan, putting his hands under the armpits again. "One, two, *three!*"

Lucy and Dan both stood up, lifting the corpse off the ground. It sagged heavily in the centre.

"Ready to swing?" she checked as they shuffled closer to the back of the garbage truck.

"Yup," replied Dan, leading the swinging motions. "One, two … *Ah, shit!*" he cried as the body tore in the middle, sending both him and Lucy off balance.

Lucy yelped in disgust, dropping the severed legs she now held and looking in horror at the writhing mass of rotting guts that lay on the road before them.

"This is too much!" yelled Dan, hurling the top half of the body into the garbage truck, sending flecks of rotten flesh through the air.

Lucy looked at the human entrails that had spilled out from the dead man's midriff and choked back the vomit. The entrails writhed with the activity of the worms feasting among them.

"This is too damned much!" said Dan, again, as he grabbed a shovel from the back of the truck and scooped up the festering remains, slinging them into the back.

"Luce?" he said, impatiently, storming over and negotiating the legs onto the shovel in a vile balancing act.

She ignored him, returning to where they'd found the body and staring at the lone squirming tapeworm left on the tar. She stepped on it, hard, twisting her foot from side to side and feeling the worm turn to pulp beneath her.

"You done?" called Dan, walking back to the front of the truck.

Lifting her foot back off, she looked at the yellow-brown mess that was left.

"Yeah," replied Lucy, "I'm done."

"Wait!" came a muffled voice from behind.

Lucy spun around, startled. Myles was limping towards her at speed from the other side of the street.

"Oh shit!" cursed Lucy, turning and hurrying back towards the truck.

"Lucy, I know that's you!" Myles shouted through his mask. "Those suits are my property! Get back here!"

She reached up, pulling open the passenger door.

"Lucy! Gimme my *fucking* suits!" yelled Myles again, closing in.

Lucy scrambled up the steps into the cockpit and threw herself into the passenger seat. "Drive, Marco!" she yelled.

"Say what?" he asked, nodding his head to the blaring heavy metal.

She leaned to pull the door closed, but Myles's hand wrapped around her forearm, dragging her from the vehicle.

"Dan!" she cried, falling hard on the asphalt.

"Lucy, I don't wanna have to do this," implored Myles. "You know that. Just gimme the goddamned suit – *please*! I'm begging you! It's mine, you know it is!"

Lucy squinted up at him, silhouetted against the bright blue sky. He was crying. That's when she saw the knife.

"I don't want this. You know that, right?" He pointed at her with the blade. "We go back a long way. I … Just … *gimme the damned suit!*" he yelled, lunging towards her.

Out of nowhere a shovel drove into the side of Myles's head with a clang, sending him plummeting to the ground. Before she could say anything, Dan lifted the shovel again and smashed it down onto Myles's skull. He struck again, and again, until Myles's brains were dashed across the street.

Lucy sat sprawled on the floor, shaking, flecks of blood covering her suit.

Dan stood up and dropped the shovel, staggering backwards. The rock music blaring from the truck stopped.

"He was gonna stab you," said Dan, swaying. "He was gonna *stab* you!"

"It's … Don't," quavered Lucy, climbing to her trembling legs. "I know he was." She took Dan's visor in her hands. "I know he was. It's OK. Shhh, it's OK."

"We need to get rid of his body," panted Dan, looking wildly around the deserted street.

"OK," said Lucy. "We can do that. Just … just be calm now. It's over."

As she turned and looked at the body again, dizziness swept through her. Dan wailed with anguish.

"I'll take the … You take the legs," said Lucy, placing a hand under each of Myles's armpits, more blood spilling onto her suit. "Dan? *Dan!*" she shouted. He was beginning to go into shock.

She dropped Myles's body and stepped up to her partner, shaking him hard. "Hey! Look at me. *Look at me!* You're OK. Right? You're OK."

She resumed her position.

"Take his legs," she ordered, fighting to keep her voice flat. "One, two, *three!*"

They staggered backwards with the decapitated body, its heat radiating through their gloves.

"Again on three," said Lucy, as they lined up level with the back of the truck.

Myles's body landed in the refuse area but rolled back towards them, his arm flopping back over the metal lip.

"Jesus Christ," winced Lucy, gagging as she flipped his hand back into the dumpster.

She grabbed the control box and hit compress. Myles's body vanished into the churning folds of humans. The squelching and cracking of flesh and bone projected over the mechanical groans of the dumpster.

140

Dan stared, transfixed. Lucy led him back to the cockpit, where she helped him up the steps.

"Buckle yourself in," she said, lifting his trembling hand onto the belt, before hopping out again and retrieving the shovel. She clipped the bloodied implement back into place on the rear of the truck and rejoined her partner, who was shaking too much to push the seat buckles together.

"I've got it," she said, leaning over and finishing it for him.

"The hell just happened?" said Marco.

"Someone tried to kill me," replied Lucy. "Please take us back to the depot, Marco."

"Gotcha!" he said, hitting *Play* on the CD deck and pulling away, singing loudly and cheerfully as Lucy's eyes glazed over.

***

"That's three hours," said Dan, lifting his head from the mattress in 403 and checking the clock on the wall.

"Thank god," heaved Lucy, tearing off her hazmat suit and taking a deep breath of unfiltered air. The sweat on her skin chilled, sending refreshing shivers across her body. That 403's gerbil was still alive had been the only mercy of the day. Lucy couldn't yet vouch for the one they'd left in Manuela's place, but there was an outside chance they'd be able to use her toilet safely if it was still alive too.

Dan slammed his palms against the wall, leaning into it, his head dipped. The half-unzipped hazmat suit hung around his waist.

"You OK?" questioned Lucy, pausing her wet-wipe shower. "Sorry. Stupid thing to ask. Of course you're not."

"I'm fine," snapped Dan, not turning around.

"What happened to Myles. That wasn't your –"

141

"I know," he interrupted, grabbing the box of wipes.

"Good. Right," said Lucy. "I mean, I know how horrible that was for you. I'm trying to say … Thank you – for saving me."

Dan paused, his cheeks pressed upward by the cleansing towels in his hands.

"I've never killed anyone before. You know that?" he said, dropping his hands to his sides and staring somewhere beyond the wall. "Five years of service, never had to do it. Always counted myself lucky." He turned to face her at last. "Are we kidding ourselves? All these bullshit systems we've put in place – waiting three hours, living in plastic suits, relying on dead people's pets to keep us alive – when all it takes is one psycho with a knife – a friend, for Christ's sake! – and that's it, game over?"

"Don't talk like that," urged Lucy. "Your systems have kept us alive." She picked up the wipes, offering him a fresh one. "We can make it through this. We've got each other, and we're going to make it through, you hear me?"

Dan snatched the pack from her and held it by his side.

"We both know we're living on luck as much as anything," said Lucy, resuming her cleansing. "But if we stay careful, if we keep our systems, maybe we'll make enough luck to see this thing through."

"Uh-huh," grunted Dan, nodding and shifting his weight. "Yup." He nodded more vigorously, his face screwing up with anger until he hurled the pack of cleaning wipes to the floor. "And what exactly *is* 'this thing', Lucy?" he snarled. "What exactly *is* that oily crap that washed up on the beach? And those spores that turned literally the entire city *yellow*? Then killed everyone? Hey? What *is* that, huh?"

He thumped his fist against the dressing table as he began to pace, jolting the antiquated jewellery, make-up, and redundant lamps from their resting places.

"And how about the weird-assed stuff that's growing everywhere? Huh?" He gestured widely with his arms as he paced. "How about the plants sprouting up in all the streets? Do they look normal to you? Lucy, do they look normal?"

Lucy continued her change-over, trying not to cry in front of him.

"We both act like we've not seen them," he fumed, "because it's just one more bullshit thing to deal with, but the truth is, we're both stuck here, guessing, and being 'lucky', while everyone else dies, and we don't mention the fact that there are brambles growing out of drains, or mould covering the bus stops, or the fact that *everything looks wet now*. What *is* that, Lucy? Hey?"

He slapped both hands out against the wall again and leaned in, exhaling heavily with his eyes closed, muttering incoherently.

Lucy calmed herself, pulling her hazmat suit back on over her legs and arms, so that just her head was exposed. Dan's heaving breaths began to subside. Lucy moved next to him, hovering under one of his outstretched arms.

"You finished?" she said, forcing him to look her in the eye.

"Yeah. Finished," he replied, blushing and flitting his eyes back to the ground.

"Good. I'll make us some dinner. Get clean and suit up. We need to eat quickly then get our masks back on."

EIGHT

The List

"Dan!" said Lucy, shaking him hard. "Dan, do you hear that?"

He jerked and sat up, disoriented. It was dawn.

"It's the signal," she cried. "We have to go!"

"The signal … Are you sure?" he said, groggily.

"*Yes*," insisted Lucy, already out of bed. "Let's go!"

They grabbed their backpacks and rushed to their bikes in the lock-up downstairs. Both of them had memorized the route to their muster point at Ashurst High School from Dan's offline map of the city. It was eight hilly miles away – a gruelling distance to cycle in a hazmat suit with fifty kilograms strapped to your back.

"Wait," said Dan as they climbed onto the bikes. "We can take these off now, right? That's what Dad's letter said – that the signal would only sound once the virus had died out?"

"You really wanna risk it? At this stage?" protested Lucy.

He considered for a moment, staring at the bike with trepidation. "You're right, not worth it. Let's go."

Lucy nodded and pushed off, with Dan following, and the two began their journey against the clock.

Marco tooted the garbage-truck horn from the opposite lane, waving cheerily as he passed by, another AC/DC classic blaring out. The man seemed completely unconcerned that his oddly dressed co-workers were cycling directly away from their pick-up point.

They passed two separate military trucks along the way, neither of which stopped or questioned them. As they got closer to the school, the route became dotted with individuals converging on the same direction by foot, all with backpacks or suitcases, some in pairs, some alone, a few with children.

As Lucy approached the school driveway, the level of fortification became apparent. Razor wire extended outward either side of the gates, while armed sentries barred the way through.

A handful of abandoned cars lined the driveway leading up to the barrier. Dozens of bicycles lay strewn across the grassy verges either side of the sidewalk.

"Watch out," said Lucy, as Dan's foot hovered above a cluster of dripping toadstools. He wobbled forward and dumped his bike in some clear grass.

Lucy followed suit, and they approached the unmasked sentries by foot.

"Name and papers?" snapped the first guard, his gritted teeth plainly visible.

Dan reached into his pocket and retrieved the letter from his father, along with their passports.

"Daniel Jeffries," stated Dan, handing the bundle over to the guard, who took the items but didn't look at them, instead consulting a printed list in his hand, flicking through its many pages and scanning each row as he went, lightly dragging a pen down the side in a tracking motion as he trawled the names.

"You're not on the list," said the guard firmly, after an uncomfortably long search, flipping back to page one and looking at them with deep suspicion. Behind him the other sentries pricked up, raising their guns slightly.

"We are, sir – please, check the letter," pressed Dan, striking a respectful tone. "We might be under my father's name?"

"Oh. You're on the *freeloader list*," spat the soldier. Well, bully for you, son. *Goldberg!*" he shouted, summoning a colleague over his shoulder. "Bring me the *freeloader list*."

This time he literally spat on the ground.

The guard consulted Dan's letter then scanned the new, significantly shorter list. "Whaddya know," he said, making no effort to conceal his contempt, "here you are."

He flipped open their passports and his cynical eyes switched between the photographs and the hazmat-suit-clad individuals before him until eventually he was satisfied. "You used to serve?" said the guard, glaring at Dan.

"Yes sir," confirmed Dan.

"Get tired of protecting your country, did you?" He crossed their names off and held out their papers, dropping the lot before Dan could reach them. "You'll need these too," he said, chucking a couple of wristbands onto the pile as Dan scrabbled to pick it all up off the ground.

"Have a *safe trip*, one and all," hissed the guard, waving them through the gates.

"Fuckin' *freeloaders*," chimed one of the other soldiers.

A row of cones led them to the sports hall, which was guarded by more unmasked soldiers. Lucy began to feel increasingly uncomfortable in the hazmat suit.

"List A or list B?" enquired the new clerk as they arrived at the school hall.

"Um," hesitated Dan, "the guy out front said we were on the freeloader li–"

"List B," interjected the clerk, cutting him off. "This way," he instructed, opening the door and pointing to a line directly opposite.

The set-up resembled airport security. There were checkpoints, and people were removing their belts and shoes and other items, and their luggage and belongings were being passed through scanners. Soldiers patrolled the inner perimeter of the hall, using gymnastic benches as vantage points. Their expressionless, helmet-clad heads protruded about a foot above the crowd.

There were dozens of Line As, but only one Line B. A floating clerk approached Dan and Lucy, and handed them each a pen and clipboard with a questionnaire attached. "Fill out this health form and hand it to the officer when you reach the end of the line. Oh, and you can take those off now," he said, pointing at their headgear. "The virus is no longer airborne."

Lucy surveyed the room as the clerk departed; a handful of individuals still wore face masks, but the vast majority had their airways exposed.

"I guess a few hundred humans will have to be our new canaries," said Lucy, lifting off her visor.

With extreme care, Dan cut away the duct tape from Lucy's gloves using a knife from his bag. She pulled the thick rubber protectives off and took the knife from Dan, delicately reciprocating.

"This is gonna get confiscated," she commented.

Once Dan's hands were liberated, Lucy resumed her de-kitting. She pulled off her mask, goggles, and hood, and loosened the chest zip on the suit. The skin around her face and chest tingled in the fresh air, and she took in several deep, unrestricted lungfuls.

She looked at Dan, whose eyes were closed, his head tilted backwards as he basked in the neon strip lights of the hall. Lucy drank in every aspect of his face.

As Line B shuffled forwards, the pair turned their attention to the health forms they'd been handed. The first few questions were standard enough – allergies, current medication, etc. – but the subsequent questions grew obscure.

"Do you have these questions too?" she asked Dan, noticing the puzzled expression on his face as he studied his form.

"About the bleeding?" he replied. "Yeah, it's weird."

Lucy surveyed the questions. *Are you a haemophiliac? Do you have any open cuts or wounds on your person? Do you suffer from nosebleeds? When was the last time you bled? If you are female, when is your next period due?*

She postponed her bewilderment and hastily filled out the form as they nudged forward again. They were next in line.

"Thank you," buzzed the seated clerk at the head of their line, snatching the clipboards from their hands. "Men to the right, women to the left." She extended a hand towards the two parallel gazebos ahead.

Dan gave Lucy's hand a fleeting squeeze – precious skin-on-skin contact – before their paths diverged.

Lucy entered her tent and the scuttling of plastic on metal signalled the curtain being pulled shut behind her. A haggard female medic stood in the centre of the tent, examining a clipboard. The woman's hair was light brown and wiry. The short curls were infused with flecks of white and extended only an inch below her ears. Dark bags hung under each eye, adding colour to her otherwise pale, wrinkly white skin.

Lucy realized the woman was wearing a protective face mask and began to panic. Desperately, she fumbled for her own face mask, while simultaneously trying to wrestle the hood back over her head.

"You don't need that," the doctor informed her.

"But you're wearing a –"

"It's for something else, a general precaution," dismissed the woman, "nothing you need to worry about. The virus is gone if that's what you're thinking. It's no longer airborne."

"So … I don't need …" hesitated Lucy, wondering why this seismic change in the city's fortunes hadn't been broadcast from the rooftops.

"No, you don't," asserted the doctor, less patiently.

Lucy lowered her visor to the floor where it rocked, the bundle of gloves, mask, and goggles inside it protruding out over the edges.

The masked doctor skimmed through Lucy's form, murmuring to herself. "Fine, fine. Take off your clothes, please," she said, glancing up.

Lucy looked around the tent, awkwardly; they were the only ones there. She unzipped the hazmat suit and slipped it down to her heels where it flopped over her rubber boots. She blushed, furiously, and pulled each boot off with a great deal of imbalance, before hastily removing the rest of the suit and her grimy 'base layer' top.

"I'll need you to remove your underwear too in a minute, but you can keep it on for now," stated the doctor, placing down the clipboard and putting on a pair of latex gloves.

Lucy's cheeks burned; she was acutely aware of her unshaven legs and the smell emanating from her freshly shed plastic skin.

"Arms out," sighed the doctor, stepping behind Lucy with a small light. She arranged Lucy's arms in a 'T'-shape before scrutinizing the tops and undersides. Lucy cringed as the doctor studied her armpit hair.

"Fine," muttered the doctor, abandoning Lucy's arms and studying the rest of her torso. Lucy kept her arms outstretched until she could support them no longer, by which time the doctor was at her ankles.

The woman returned to Lucy's head and meticulously examined her scalp, prising strands of hair apart and probing the skin beneath. "I need you to take off your bra and underwear now," she said, making another note on her clipboard.

Lucy obliged, slipping off her underwear. She stared straight ahead, willing the examination to be over.

"Yes, yes," mumbled the doctor before facing Lucy once again. "Last bit, sorry. I need you to lie on the bench and open your legs."

Lucy did a cartwheel of embarrassment in her head. She tried to act casual as she lay on her back, staring at the tent ceiling, while the woman shone a flashlight directly onto her vagina.

"Alright, you can put your underwear on again, but I need you to keep your midriff exposed and lie back down on the bed when you're ready."

Lucy turned her back to the doctor and quickly pulled her underwear back on, before lying down on the bench as instructed. The doctor approached wearing a pair of protective goggles and handed Lucy a pair too.

"Put these on for me and look straight up at the ceiling. This will only take a moment."

Lucy put the goggles on as the doctor wheeled over a trolley. The device on top resembled a lamp, but in place of the bulb there was a thin silver rod about the length of a pen.

"Just lean back and relax for me," instructed the doctor. "Count aloud to ten. You'll feel a slight pinch, but the vaccination won't take long."

Lucy leant back and opened her mouth. "One, two," she counted, nervously, as a warm sensation spread across her abdomen.

By the time she got to eight, the heat was intense and starting to burn painfully.

"Nine," she said, choking back the tears and gagging with disbelief. "Ten!" she cried with a gasp, clenching her teeth as the excruciating sensation continued for several more seconds.

"OK, you're all done," stated the doctor, reaching down and passing Lucy her top.

Lucy pulled the garment over her head and down to her burning abdomen, cradling the area with her hands.

"The burning will pass within an hour or so," commented the doctor, handing Lucy her backpack. The woman slid back the exit curtain to reveal the rear of the sports hall where Dan stood waiting.

"You'll need to finish dressing out there I'm afraid, we're on a very tight schedule," clipped the doctor.

"My suit," said Lucy, pointing to the crumpled mass.

"You don't need that anymore," sighed the woman, "and we can't permit it on the train I'm afraid."

Lucy shuffled towards the exit, her weighty backpack slung over one shoulder, a hand still nursing her abdomen. The gazebo curtain closed behind her. A soldier stepped forward and affixed a green band to Lucy's wrist.

"Luce, are you OK?" said Dan, quickly crossing over to her, also wearing a green wristband. He gently lifted the backpack from her shoulder and set it on the floor, rummaging through the contents and pulling out a pair of jeans. He held each leg open for her to dazedly step into. "Luce?" he asked again, guiding her hands to the waist button. Muscle memory kicked in and she absently fastened the jeans while Dan negotiated sneakers onto her feet.

"I think I've just been sterilized," she uttered, hearing the words coming out of her mouth as if they were said by a stranger, her eyes falling down on Dan, who looked up from one knee, aghast.

"You two, hurry up!" barked a soldier. "Get your asses onto the transport if you wanna make that train!"

A commotion broke out a few rows along from them.

"Help! Somebody, please! Please help!" cried a distraught woman, imploring her neighbouring civilians who continued to back away.

"Ma'am, please," said a soldier, trying to contain the situation, but the lady was having none of it.

"Go to hell!" yelled the woman. "Scott! Scott!" she called out, reaching out to a man not far from her who was being separately restrained.

A set of troops encircled the woman, some facing her, others facing the rest of the hall to ensure there was no further dissent. A terrified young child clung to the woman's leg, burying his infant face in her thigh.

"Listen to them, honey, it's gonna be OK," pleaded the man, presumably her husband, while trying to shrug off the firm grips of the soldiers either side of him. "Jonah, Jonah buddy, it's gonna be alright, OK? Daddy's gonna be fine," he insisted, addressing the young boy, who continued to hide.

Lucy's eyes tracked down to the man's left leg, where his pant leg had been rolled up to the knee, revealing a bloodied bandage around his shin.

"Ma'am, please," interjected a soldier. "I'm going to order my troops to stand down so you can say goodbye, but I need you to remain calm, do you understand?"

"I am *not* leaving him here!" cried the woman, channelling her distress and anger directly at the officer.

"Then none of you will be able to travel," replied the officer, patience waning as the evacuation deadline loomed closer. "Those are your options. It's you and the child or none of you. I ain't going on the train, so it makes no difference to me. It's your life. But you gotta decide right now."

"Please, let me talk to my wife," begged the man from outside the circle. The officer begrudgingly signalled his troops to release him. The man rushed forwards to his wife and gripped her desperately in his arms, the two openly weeping. He broke off the embrace and took his wife's face in his hands, staring her straight in the eyes. "I'll find you when this is all over. I promise," he insisted.

"Scott," she pleaded, but he cut her off.

"Take Jonah, and do what we all need you to do. I can get by here, but I won't be able to live with myself if you two don't get on that train because of me," he replied.

The wife shook her head, sobbing. She pressed her forehead into her husband's.

"Professor, we need to go. I'm sorry," interrupted the officer.

The man kissed his wife then knelt down beside his son, turning the terrified boy around to face him. Fresh tear tracks lined the boy's puffy young cheeks as he stared at his father wide-eyed with love and confusion.

"Jonah, your mom's a really important person, you know that? And Daddy needs you to look after her while you're both away. Daddy's gotta do some stuff here, but he'll catch you up as soon as he can. Can you promise me you'll look after Mommy until then?"

The little boy nodded, his unchanged expression showing how little of the situation he comprehended.

The man gave his boy and his wife one last hug before a soldier led him away and out of sight. The mother and son were swiftly ushered away through the hall's main exit, with two soldiers helping the grieving woman to walk while a third carried her child in his arms.

Ripples of uncertainty spread across the rest of the hall, as anxious evacuees tried to fathom the precise reasons for the man's eviction, wondering if they were next.

"Alright, let's turn it around!" shouted the ranking officer, galvanizing his stalled troops and clerks back into action.

As they stepped into the main corridor, following the other processed evacuees out into the rear parking lot, the pain in Lucy's abdomen flared up, making her bend over. Dan placed a protective arm around her shoulder, shielding her from the jostling crowd. She glanced around as they moved; many of the women her age bore similar signs of agony, but the older women seemed unaffected.

A row of empty troop-carrier trucks stretched out across the lot. Green-wristbanded people climbed into the backs, sending up their backpacks first then clambering in with the help of those already on board.

"Lists A one through nine this way, list B that way!" announced an officer through a megaphone, repeating the message as people streamed by.

Lucy counted about a dozen trucks in all as Dan steered them towards the lone B-lorry at the far end of the line.

Dan threw their backpacks in and helped Lucy up the steps. She swayed at the top, prompting an older woman to leap up and help her into a seat.

Lucy looked around at the other occupants of the truck; they ranged in age and ethnicity, but all had the same slightly shifty look and tended to avoid eye contact. Perhaps the word "freeloader" was echoing around their heads too.

"Move out!" came the order further up, followed by the sound of engines starting. Their vehicle sprang to life with a rumble and splutter, shaking its occupants then settling down into a juddering idle. The other trucks could be heard pulling away one after another while the last of truck B's passengers were loaded.

Lucy stared out of the open back as they pulled away, passing the razor-wire boundary. Two Humvees with mounted gun turrets tagged on behind them, obscuring her view of the school's shrinking American flag as it rippled defiantly in the breeze.

***

Lucy started to recognize certain buildings as they got closer to the train station.

With a lurch the engine suddenly cranked up several gears and the truck plunged forwards, sending its passengers jostling into one another. One of the Humvees pulled out and overtook them, its navigator pointing to something ahead and shouting as they disappeared from view.

Masses of people began to appear in the truck's wake, standing amid uncollected bodies. Some protestors wore masks, others had their faces exposed, some had backpacks, others held baseball bats. Razor wire had been deployed along the sidewalks, keeping the angry crowd at bay as the convoy passed through. Ground troops hastily closed the makeshift razor gate as the last Humvee passed through. The crowd's shouting was incoherent, but its anger was palpable. There weren't just thousands of them, there were tens of thousands.

Truck B came to a halt amid a protective circle of two hundred troops who stood between them and the wire. Soldiers bellowed at Lucy and her fellow occupants to get the hell out.

She and Dan threw their backpacks out of the truck and leapt after them, Lucy's abdomen burning with the impact of concrete underfoot. As she and Dan scrabbled to refasten their bags, specific chants from the crowd became audible.

"Let us on the fucking train!" came a cry from nearby, which was met with roars of approval and echoes of cursing directed at the evacuees.

"What about our goddamn *rights*? What about our *rights*?" came another cry from behind the wire.

"Come on, keep it moving!" yelled a soldier, giving Lucy a shove towards the station entrance. All along the way soldiers yelled at them, urging them forward through the open barriers and ticket hall and out towards the train.

The platform was rammed with people from the other trucks, all hurrying to find their carriage. "Truck B right ahead!" screamed a soldier, straining to be heard above the crowd as Lucy's pace slowed, unsure where to turn. Dan grabbed her hand, pulling her straight ahead and onto the carriage steps.

"Keep going! Move along inside!" came more bellowing from the soldiers below, furiously directing the passengers further into the carriages as more approached.

Theirs was the nearest and last carriage on the train. Lucy and Dan climbed the stairs to the upper deck where they flung themselves into the closest seats. The two turned and stared out of the window fearfully as the hoards of angry and desperate people surrounding the station began to escalate their protests.

Lucy's eye moved to the razor wire directly ahead where a man was pulling off his shirt. He tore it in two and wrapped it around each hand before taking hold of the barrier and prising the metal spirals apart, slowly edging forwards in-between the wire.

"Get *back*!" shouted a nearby soldier, Lucy reading his lips through the thick glass, but the topless man didn't listen. The soldier smashed his rifle butt into the man's jaw, sending him crashing backwards, the wire springing back viciously as the man's grip slackened with the impact. He fell to the ground, blood immediately leaking from the scores of razor cuts across his body.

A retaliatory bottle flew out from the midst of the crowd and smashed into the soldier's helmet, sending shards of glass into his cheek. The soldier reeled backward as two colleagues closed in to provide reinforcement.

The first warning shots rang out. Lucy's eye darted over to a jeep where a marshal stood atop the hood, the recently fired pistol in his right hand pointing directly at the sky, a megaphone in his left hand.

"This is your final warning!" cried the marshal. "There is no more room on the train, but rations are available to you. The virus is over, the city will be restored soon. Disperse immediately or we will use lethal force."

As the marshal lowered his megaphone and turned to climb off the jeep, a fresh gunshot rang out. He pivoted on the spot, off balance, as the bullet blasted into his shoulder, sending him crashing to the ground. A whistle sounded and the vehicle's gun turret launched into action. The gunner fired suppression patterns into the crowd, sending the mob sprawling outwards as they trampled and crushed each other in flight, while tear-gas grenades exploded underfoot.

But as the plumes of gas spread among the crowd, a breach formed in the barrier. The wire to Lucy's right had been cut, and desperate citizens now surged through the rupture. The nearest turret began to spin around to halt the unstoppable tide, but it was too late: the crowd was among them now. The gunner pulled out his revolver and began to pick off advancing individuals, many of whom fell immediately, not being armed at all.

The adjacent Humvee reversed suddenly, wiping out two civilians. But before the gunner could engage the oncoming masses, a hail of bullets burst through the tear-gas smokescreen. An armoured police vehicle surged through the perimeter, firing at soldiers and civilians indiscriminately.

The wire wrapped itself around the careering police truck. The vehicle strained as the razors bit into its tyres and mangled around the axle, bringing it to a halt. But the truck had quashed a large section of fence, which the mob now poured through, immediately overwhelming the only remaining turret gunner.

A scrawny male civilian with his hood pulled up leapt onto the now-vacant turret and attempted to retrain it against the military, but was immediately shot down by the ground-level troops.

As the soldiers engaged the advancing mob in two-way gunfire, a third breach appeared in the perimeter and thousands more began to pour through the gap, knocking each other over and trampling the fallen underfoot as they raced towards the train.

A second police riot vehicle raced into the fray and a dozen self-styled militia men poured out onto the concourse wielding a mixture of handguns, rifles, and machine guns.

Through the stuttering gunfire, shouting, and engine revs came a second whistle, and the train lurched forwards. The mob spilled out onto the platform and began running towards the train.

"Jesus Christ, they're gonna board us!" cried a terrified man a few rows along. The whole carriage lined the windows, staring in terror as hundreds of people poured onto the concourse, all running in their direction. Some quickly began shedding their backpacks and weapons in a bid to run faster.

As the twelve-carriage, double-decker behemoth slugged forwards, the mob began to close in on Lucy and Dan's carriage.

"Help! Please help us! Wait!" cried a man so earnestly he could be heard through the thick glass of the upper deck. He was almost level with their carriage door now, closely followed by dozens more, all doggedly chasing the accelerating train. His arm extended out towards the carriage railing, a look of profound urgency widening his desperate eyes as his fingers homed in on the rail.

"Wait! No!" cried the man, before a burst of gunfire spurted out from the lower deck. He vanished from sight, along with the runners nearest him.

More gunshots; the deck below continued to fire. Lucy pressed her face into the glass, trying to see what was happening, but the window frame blocked her view.

"Lucy!" called Dan a little way behind her. She rushed over and joined him at the rear door, which was the end of the train. Together they peered out of the circular, hatch-like window and watched in horror. Bodies lay strewn across the concrete in race formation, dotted out like a track-and-field massacre. Behind them was a growing group of people arriving onto the platform only to realize the train had gone.

Lucy stared at the mob members; they were ordinary people, arms hanging limply by their sides, gaunt faces gazing back at her in disbelief as the train pulled clear of the platform.

The locomotive continued to gather speed, the sounds of gunfire and chaos giving way to the clatter of the engine as it cleared the besieged station and abandoned what remained of the city.

NINE

End of the Line

Lucy awoke the next morning in the position she'd fallen asleep in, wrapped up in Dan's arms. His chin rested on her head as she used his torso as a pillow.

San Francisco seemed a distant memory as the train snaked its way through the lunar landscape of the Rocky Mountains. But the boulder-strewn expanse was being invaded by a new colour: covering the dark, rusty landscape were patches of the palest blue. Some sort of glistening moss or lichen was spreading across the region. Lucy felt a wave of nausea and guilt as the station scenes flashed back, and she pressed her head further into Dan's chest, forcing her eyes shut. She couldn't deal with it; not now. Maybe not ever.

Over the course of the day the train climbed the Jurassic hillscape, at times ascending into the cloud line where the sun's light was scattered and reflected from either side of the carriage in a cold, bright, halogen shade of white, the bottom of the mountains disappearing off into the mist below.

Lucy's nose caught the scent of someone else's meal from a few seats ahead. As she walked to the luggage rack at the far end she noticed that other people were charging their phones and laptops using the train's sockets. She rifled through her and Dan's backpacks, extracting their phones, chargers, and some food.

"For you," she said, returning to her seat and placing a tin of fruit in front of her partner. Like her, he hadn't eaten since they'd boarded yesterday. Dan nodded, passively, his gaze fixed on the outside.

Lucy opened his tin of peaches and left it in front of him with a fork, before attending to her own portion. He silently ate his lot before retreating into sleep again. Lucy cleared away and put the phones on to charge.

Several more hours passed during which Lucy contemplated their arrival in DC, hopeful that Dan's reunion with his father would help him with the loss of his sister, Kim. But Lucy herself was still reeling from the loss of Cassie. With no one to talk to – the other passengers were largely silent – she retrieved a notepad and pen from her luggage and began to write.

Barring a few particularly pubescent weeks as an early teen, she'd never regarded diary-keeping as a worthwhile pursuit. But now it seemed appropriate – important, even – to document all that she could remember from the last two weeks. What had happened, who they'd seen, what they'd done. She tried to be as objective as possible, aware that it might one day form part of a historical record.

And so she penned it all, beginning with Cassie's birthday drinks, through to Dan stockpiling goods that night, to the extortion and execution at the drugstore, to their neighbour dying just yards away from them, to the canaries, and becoming garbage-truck undertakers.

Her prose quickly became bullet points, such was her determination to cover every event and every departure from what had, up until recently, been her normal life.

We were attacked on garbage duty. Myles, my boss, came at me with a knife but Dan saved me.* We made it to the evac train.* Kim died – we found out by letter.* I think the army sterilized me.*

Events occurred to her out of sequence. The notebook quickly became littered with asterisks leading to separate pages where stub entries would be properly embellished.

She paused, the pen hovering above the page, and stared at her own words. *I think the army sterilized me.* The permanence of it, were it to be true, began to dawn on her. She flipped the notebook and turned it upside down, so that the back cover opened like it was the front page, and she began a new section.

If I die, and this book is found, it's about my life. I'm writing it because I need to. This back part is about my childhood; it's about life before everything went wrong – although lots of that went wrong anyway, and I'm not sure I'll ever understand why. The front part is about what happened after the satellites failed. If I am never able to have children, I hope at least I can pass on my story.

Returning to the front of the notepad, she closed it, exhausted. She'd been writing non-stop for hours. She stretched her hand out several times; the muscles ached from gripping the pen. For all the cramp in her hand, some of the tightness in her chest at least had eased; it was a starting point.

She turned to Dan, who had pulled a sleeping mask over his eyes. His head was turned towards the window and a thin silvery tear-trail glistened on his cheek.

She looked at him and contemplated his handsome features: the stubble lining his jowl, the tiny furry hairs on the sides of his ears, the creases in the skin across his forehead. She missed him.

***

As the train gradually descended back towards sea level, Colorado's mountainous terrain gave way to fields infused with pale blue reeds.

Around mid-afternoon the train slowed and a long, curving concrete platform came into view. It was speckled with more of the pale 'lichen' Lucy had seen earlier. Dan stirred at the change of pace and lifted his sleeping mask up. Lucy placed her hand on his, relishing the touch of his skin, and the pair looked out at the small group of people waiting on the platform.

Two expectant passengers stood side by side awaiting the train: a middle-aged man and woman, both smartly dressed and each with a wheeled suitcase. A lone police officer stood with them, his stern face, which was augmented by a thick handlebar moustache, jutting out from beneath a cowboy hat adorned with a sheriff's badge. Here, there were no angry crowds, no soldiers, no razor wire; just the prim couple who were now preparing to board one of the A-list carriages further ahead.

The train slowed to a crawl but kept moving. The couple began to keep pace with it, realizing it wasn't going to stop.

Lucy watched as the cop grabbed the woman's suitcase and threw it into the foremost A-carriage. He shouted instructions to the couple while grabbing the man's bag. The prim woman raised a hand to her abdomen – Lucy wondered if she had been sterilized too. She looked too old, surely?

A uniformed arm extended out from the carriage door and grabbed the woman's hand, pulling her on board, then reappeared to grab the anxiously jogging man too. The sheriff hurled the second suitcase on board then slowed to a walk, watching as the train pulled away, giving a reciprocal salute to the soldier on the train before turning on his heel.

Lucy craned her neck as they passed him, watching the cop walk back towards his car, alone.

"'Scuse, Luce," said Dan, breaking his vow of silence and edging out from his window seat, heading down the aisle towards the next carriage.

When he returned, a few minutes later, he said, "I overheard some of the A-listers talking next door. One of them was saying he had evidence that the virus was terrorist in origin, but the other was saying that her lab had eliminated that as a possibility because the samples they'd collected weren't terrestrial."

"So?" frowned Lucy.

"So I asked them where the bathroom was," said Dan.

Ah, so he was still there. He didn't smile, but a flicker of humour was a good sign.

"It's two carriages along, by the way," he finished, squeezing back into his seat and setting about unwrapping a Twinkie bar he'd pulled from his bag. "Ours is out of order. Oh, and that was it! The thing everyone was calling 'the virus' – it's not a virus. Apparently it's more like bacteria or something. Sounded like pro … carrot?"

"Prokaryote?" suggested Lucy.

Dan tore a chunk out of the Twinkie bar. "That sounds about right."

Convulsive

"Two carriages along, yeah? I'll be back in a minute," said Lucy, setting off up the train.

The doors swept aside with a pneumatic hiss. She put her hands out onto the walls ahead to stabilize her transition between carriages as the train rocked.

Unlike her own carriage, the first A-list car had much more of a conversational buzz about it. People had gathered in small clusters as best they could, some sitting, others standing around the rows in discussion with each other. Passengers were crossing in and out of the next carriage along with impunity as the porous exchanges continued, so Lucy's entrance broke no unwritten rules; no one gave her so much as a second glance.

In the immediate row to her left a pair slept. To her right a more industrious pair were engrossed in note-making, one typing furiously on a laptop, the other feverishly annotating some sketches on paper.

She was about to continue down the aisle when two individuals entered at the opposite end of the carriage.

"Can I have your attention please, everyone," declared the foremost new arrival, loudly. She was an academic-looking woman of Indian heritage. The woman looked to be in her mid-forties. She wore a smart black cardigan over a plain, light grey top. Her dark hair was centre-parted and stopped an inch above her shoulders, framing her tan-coloured skin.

The man standing next to her was a good decade older, with silvery-grey hair that had receded halfway across his pale head. He wore a beige blazer with black dog-tooth patterning, and rimless rectangular glasses.

"Apologies for the late running of this briefing," said the woman. "Carriage A7 had a lot of questions, as I'm sure will you. My name is Professor Rupali Sheraton. I will be relaying the information we have from NASA. My colleague, Doctor Phillip Tauro, will then be briefing you on the nature of the pandemic."

The standing occupants of the carriage quickly returned to their seats and pulled out notepads and tablets.

"We can't be sure exactly when this began, but what I'm about to outline took place primarily within a forty-eight-hour period," continued the professor. "We believe the satellite failures were caused by a bacterial cloud that was drawn into Earth's gravity. I say 'bacterial' but really that's by way of analogy. They were single-celled organisms – to begin with. Our hypothesis is that the organisms were able to metabolize one of the components of the Solar Array Drive Mechanisms in the satellites, resulting in critical failure.

"While the organisms were proliferating on the satellites – initially undetected – gravity pulled the rest of this transparent cloud into low orbit, where we believe it contaminated an astronaut's suit during a spacewalk. The astronaut then unwittingly brought the pathogen aboard the International Space Station, where a crew handover had been going on for several weeks.

"The organisms interacted with samples in the space station's labs, resulting in new variants. The crew began to notice these anomalous results and reported samples corrupting, overflowing, and generally undergoing rapid change – but they could not identify the cause.

"The return crew boarded the Soyuz shuttle as scheduled and departed for Earth. While the Soyuz crew were in transit, the remaining astronauts aboard the ISS all experienced fatal cardiac events within minutes of each other. We received no further signal.

"We then lost contact with the Soyuz capsule, which wasn't discovered until twelve hours later. It had splashed down in the Gulf of Aden, way off course. This was the moment the pathogen transitioned from space to Earth – contaminating our oceans.

"The Soyuz recovery was probably one of the last things you saw on the news. We took samples from inside the shuttle, which were flown to labs in San Fran. We never found the crew.

"It was shortly after the Soyuz was located that the satellites failed completely. First we lost satellites over China and India, then over Central Europe, and finally over North America. This pattern is consistent with the hypothesis that the initial contamination came from a gravity-drawn cloud. At this point I'll hand over to Doctor Tauro."

The doctor took a half-step forward and cleared his throat as Professor Sheraton vacated the spot.

"Good afternoon, everyone. As Rupali said, this thing seems to have arrived from space. That's as much as we know in terms of its origins, but it tells us something about its properties. It's an extremophile, for starters, which is going to make it hard to kill. Secondly, it is *uniquely* aggressive, owing to a number of factors that I'll come to.

"It is a new domain of life – the fourth domain. Its relationship with DNA is unlike anything observed on Earth. For now we are simply referring to it as 'D4'."

The balding doctor cleared his throat again and rocked on his heels.

"We've tried to sequence its genome and have so far failed. After numerous attempts, and after ruling out several other hypotheses, my team and I began to suspect the presence of non-terrestrial bases in its DNA. That is to say, we suspected our tests were failing because they were encountering something that was not part of the terrestrial GATC set, and therefore something we were not hitherto equipped to measure.

"We devised a new test, and I'm pleased – or startled, depending on your perspective – to announce that we have indeed identified two new base pairs. We're not yet certain of their properties or variants, but we consider this definitive proof that the pathogen is extraterrestrial. For now, we're calling the new bases S and Z, in honour of the Soyuz and ISS crews.

"We believe that D4 has similarities to the CRISPR Cas9 mechanisms seen in some terrestrial bacteria. It seems able to assimilate the DNA of any species it interacts with, and appropriate elements into its own code. Crucially, however, it uses this as a weapon, rather than a form of defence. Our most recent findings suggest that the S-Z base pairs function as 'spacers', or 'links' between appropriated sets of terrestrial DNA. We believe the S-Z bases are the key to its genetic plasticity.

"What I want to stress to you is that, from what we have observed so far, this pathogen has very little in the way of its own identity. D4 is a life form defined not by its manifestations, but by its mechanisms. It is a *process*, and regarding it as such will be the key to our fight."

The doctor paused, allowing the furious typing and note-making to continue until the audience had caught up.

"Our investigations were frustrated by power disruption," he continued, "and latterly by loss of key personnel, but we hope to resume the research in Washington. In terms of evidence, my lab took samples from the ocean, the spores that blew inland, the new fauna that emerged, and from the carcasses of terrestrial mammals that had succumbed to D4 – including humans.

"We have also discovered instances of new species: D4 variants of terrestrial mammals. The vast majority of genetic material in these new species appears to be terrestrial DNA, but those terrestrial sequences are regulated by D4's S-Z bases.

"In essence, D4 scavenges for genetic parts and splices them together. The resulting progeny vary wildly in their viability and the extent to which 'new' DNA is expressed. Each new D4 generation remains identifiable through the presence of S-Z bases, and through their unique reproductive characteristics, despite them exhibiting traits from the organisms they've preyed upon.

"Reproduction indeed appears to be the key to D4's success," continued the doctor. "Regardless of size or terrestrial genetic composition, it reproduces through fission. Progeny emerge fully matured. We call these occurrences 'massive respecialization events'. In these MREs, the entire pathogen appears to return to a despecialized state – a globule. This globule then spontaneously *re*specializes into one or more fully formed organisms, in which appropriated genes are expressed.

"We believe that MREs have enabled the pathogen to perform evolutionary leapfrogs. Three weeks ago this thing was basically a bacterium, and already it's amassed enough cellular material to form organisms millions of times that size. It's evolution at a rate we are not prepared for."

More murmurs from the audience.

"However, as it forms increasingly complex organisms, D4's breeding cycle slows, bringing it more in line with what we're used to on Earth. In other words, an S-Z bacterium may take minutes, but an S-Z sperm whale will take months to gestate. That sort of scale. Hence the number of S-Z-positive mammals we've encountered is vastly smaller than, say, the number of spores you saw in San Francisco.

"Presumably availability of food is the greatest rate-limiting factor in its breeding cycle. If it evolves to eat more, faster, it will likely reproduce faster too, and continue to grow in size. An urgent question for us, then, is: *how* are they consuming enough matter to sustain such growth? We think part of the answer lies in D4's ability to switch from behaving as a single-celled organism to a multicellular one, much like a slime mould. This is possible when D4 takes liquid form – what we've dubbed 'Gen Water'."

The doctor paused, removing his glasses and cleaning the lenses with the hem of his shirt before replacing them, ignoring a raised hand from the audience.

"Gen Water is a source both of food and of new genetic material. We believe D4 kills its host then triggers a rapid digestion process. We don't fully understand the mechanism yet. It could be something akin to an enzyme, or perhaps it utilizes something within the host. We don't know. But what we *do* know is that, once fully digested, the carcass disintegrates and disperses. It does *not* go straight into an MRE. Each carcass is transformed into Gen Water. That liquid then disperses, and can be co-opted by another D4 organism undergoing an MRE.

"In our lab we took two samples. The first was taken from a D4 creature which had looked almost identical to a terrestrial cat before it began to despecialize. It turned to Gen Water and began to form a globule – a precursor to mass respecialization. We exposed the D4 'cat' globule to *inactive* Gen Water taken from a human cadaver. There was an almost magnetic attraction between the samples. The human Gen Water was drawn into the cat globule, which grew proportionally to how much we fed it. But the progeny were not half-cat, half-human, as the ratios would suggest. The globule yielded a dozen smaller creatures more akin to salamanders. Our interpretation of this is that the D4 'cat' may have been exposed to salamander DNA during a previous MRE. The genes were stored in its genetic library, dormant, until the S-Z bases 'chose' to express them in this particular respecialization."

"What happened to them?" asked a woman. "To the D4 'salamanders'?"

"They attacked each other," replied Dr Tauro. "Possibly a consequence of being trapped in a confined space, but we can't be sure at this stage. We terminated the surviving samples."

"If D4 can turn to Gen Water, does that mean the water's alive?" asked a man near the front.

"Yes and no," replied the doctor. "You could almost think of Gen Water as stem cells awaiting activation. It's basically an energy-rich DNA soup, which has the ability to become a functional D4 organism – but we don't yet know how or at what point it becomes 'alive'. We also don't understand how D4 is able to transform both organic and inorganic matter into Gen Water."

Several more hands went up.

"From what you've said, Doctor Tauro, it sounds like the only time they can feed is during reproduction?" asked a man near Lucy.

"That's the only time we've observed so far," replied the doctor, "but that could simply be because we induced it. We have yet to observe feeding in the wild. But I'm sure many of you are already sensing the opportunity this knowledge presents; if we can identify a DNA sequence that is *toxic* to D4, we could potentially engineer a virus to replicate *in* the Gen Water. It could be a way of eradicating the pathogen."

Another hand went up.

"Yes?" said Professor Sheraton, stepping forward to share the questioning burden.

"The Gen Water process – where an organic host is broken down – is that what happened to the crew of the Soyuz capsule?" asked a greying woman three rows from Lucy.

"We believe so, yes," replied the professor. "We suspect there is a link between the number of D4 cells and the speed the victim degrades. The Soyuz was an extremely confined space, with a heat catalyst. Our hypothesis is that the crew were degraded within the twelve hours it took to locate the capsule, and that their Gen Water contaminated the ocean. Our fear is that we're now seeing this heat catalyst effect on a global scale; we've lost the contrails from air traffic and it's pushing average temperatures up."

A dozen hands shot up again, but this time Doctor Tauro intervened, raising both of his palms in surrender. "Thank you for your time, everyone. This is the eighth consecutive briefing we've had to do, so perhaps you'll grant us leave for now. We're both situated in carriage A1, so please do come and find us later today if you wish to discuss your thoughts further. Thank you again."

As the doctor and professor departed, the carriage erupted in conversation. Lucy took half a step forwards, but the man and woman immediately before her had each leaned in from their aisle seats and were engaged in animated discussion. She hesitated.

"Can I help you?" snapped the man, suddenly glaring at her.

"Sorry ... I was ..." stumbled Lucy.

"Don't apologize to him," said the woman, jumping in. "Just because our entire understanding of life science has been turned on its head, doesn't mean there's not a place for manners. I'm Jean. You are?"

She took the woman's proffered hand. "Lucy."

"Nice to meet you, Lucy. You're from the carriage behind, I take it?" the woman enquired.

The man snorted derisively.

"This is Mohammed," continued Jean. "As you can probably tell from his social skills, he's a computer scientist."

"Don't shun my kind, we're the ones who can get mankind back on track. Ninety per cent reduction in population means tiny labour force means we need automated machines. And automated machines need this guy," he said, pointing to himself with both thumbs. "But how about you, Carriage B, what are you for?"

Lucy blinked, taken aback.

"What am I *for*?" she repeated.

"That's what I said, isn't it?" snapped the man.

"Mo, don't be a jackass," interrupted Jean.

"What? We live in a binary world. You're either useful or you're not," he shrugged.

"And you're either an asshole, or you're not," replied Lucy, regretting her words immediately.

Jean laughed.

"True," agreed Mohammed, to her surprise. "But your carriage could have been filled with medics. That's all I'm saying."

"Oh do shut up, Mo. The whole premise of this train is abhorrent," reproached Jean. "It's revolting that we even have to reduce human worth to utility like this. If the new world were populated by the likes of us alone, I'm not sure it's a place I'd want to live."

"Are you going past or what?" Mohammed snarked, addressing Lucy once again.

"Uh, yeah. The bathroom's this way, right, Jean?" asked Lucy.

"Yes dear, down the stairs at the end," the woman replied.

Lucy nodded and gave her an awkward smile, then headed to the end of the carriage and down the stairs.

***

As she stepped out of the tiny washroom, the train began to slow again. Lucy expected to see another provincial station coming into view alongside the tracks, but there was only a patchwork quilt of forest and fields, turning a hue of dark purple as the sun departed.

After a minute of deceleration the train came to a complete stop, jolting slightly as the brakes locked into position. As Lucy passed back through the A-carriage, murmurs spread among the passengers, all craning to see out of their windows.

"This must be some sort of mistake," insisted one. "We're not supposed to be stopping at all now until DC, that's what they said, right? That's what they said?" repeated the woman, looking to her fellow passengers for reassurance.

A soldier hastily ascended the stairs, emerging from the deck below. He hurried through A7, pushing past Lucy and the other folk blocking the aisles. Ignoring their bombardment of questions, he pressed on to the next carriage. Lucy watched him hasten towards the front of the train until misaligned doors obscured him from view.

She decided to get back to Dan, politely weaving through the crowded aisles of A7 and A8 until she reached Carriage B. The taboo of silence had been broken by the unexplained stop, and scared B-listers were at last talking to one another openly.

"This can't be good," said a lone man, his eyes wrought with fear. "I mean, look at what happened in San Francisco, right? First the satellites, then the virus. Now this!" He gestured to the wilderness around them.

"I'm sure they'll get us moving again," assured a woman close by, softly.

"Ah, what do *you* know? You're stuck here with the rest of us," said the man.

"I saw a soldier walking that way," interjected Lucy. "I think he's gone to talk to the driver, so I think they're on it."

She smiled, nervously, realizing all eyes in the carriage were suddenly on her. She hurried away from the threshold to the A-listers and back towards her row, keeping her head down. Dan stood in the aisle, next to their seats.

"What do you think?" Lucy whispered, leaning into him.

177

"No idea," he whispered back, "but stay close until we're moving again."

"OK," she replied, giving a reassuring grin to a nervous-looking child a few rows ahead, who quickly looked away. Lucy retook her seat and scoured the twilight for clues.

After fifteen minutes the intercom crackled into life.

"Attention all passengers, this is Lieutenant Gladwell. We have been advised by HQ to discontinue our journey to DC. We have received information that the capital has been compromised, and that we are to await further instructions. We will bring you more information when we have it, but for now we will be staying here."

The intercom mic clicked off, giving way to an upswell of voices demanding answers and proclaiming conclusions. As the bickering continued, the last of the daylight faded behind the mountains, and night moved in on their position.

"We're in the wrong carriage for information," said Dan, casting his eyes around the scared-looking B-listers. "Someone in the other coaches will know the real reason we've stopped. They must do, otherwise they wouldn't be on board."

At that moment the compartment door hissed open and the lieutenant entered, flanked by two other soldiers.

"What do you think it means?" the lieutenant snarled in response to an anxious passenger.

The soldiers hastened through the carriage and down to the deck below without a word, brushing aside those who got in their way. Lucy tiptoed over to the stairwell and tried in vain to catch some of the hushed conversation. The only noise to reach her was the clicking of weapons being loaded.

The two soldiers who had flanked the lieutenant reappeared, now fully clad in combat uniforms. Helmets and flak jackets on, and assault rifles in hand, they made their way back through the aisle and into the next carriage, their guise and weaponry pre-emptively clearing their path.

Lucy retook her seat next to Dan, who was facing the window. She studied his reflection in the glass of their cocoon, watching as his eyes tracked from side to side and trying to follow his gaze.

A commotion in the adjoining carriage pricked Lucy's ears. The doors hissed open and a terrified, bedraggled elderly man stumbled forwards. Gripping the geriatric by the scruff of his suit, a stronger man of around forty coerced his ward forwards. Without thinking, Lucy stepped out into the aisle, blocking the pair's way.

"Who are you and what are you doing with him?" she asked, directly challenging the strong man.

"Lucy!" hissed Dan, rising from his seat.

"I'm saving our lives is what I'm doing!" the man shouted back, his biceps showing through his navy blue chequered shirt, a dark brown beard embellishing his round face. "Now move!" he cried, jostling the old man forward again.

Lucy edged back a few paces.

"Luce," Dan pleaded.

She ignored him. With a heavy sigh Dan addressed the bearded man.

"Tell us what you're doing with him," Dan stated, approaching the edge of their row.

"Jesus fucking Christ, you people aren't even supposed to be on this train!" cried the assailant.

"What's going on?" growled the lieutenant as his heavy footsteps echoed up the stairs.

The old man mumbled incoherently, sobbing as he hung from his adversary's grip, the soles of his feet barely touching the floor.

"He's bleeding!" yelled the bearded man to the lieutenant. "You know what we have to do, sir," he added, lowering his voice.

"Please … Please, it'll pass, I know it will," spluttered the old man, reaching again for his handkerchief as a hacking cough took hold. When he pulled the handkerchief away, the white cotton was speckled with blood.

"Oh my god, put him down, he needs help!" cried Lucy, aghast.

"He needs to get the hell off this train, is what he needs!" replied the bearded aggressor. "You know what's coming for us if we don't," stated the man, addressing the lieutenant.

The lieutenant said nothing for a moment. With his eyes cast downwards he gave the smallest of nods.

"Come on, then," said the vigilante, shoving the old man forwards. Lucy and Dan parted, stunned by the lieutenant's endorsement of the situation.

The lieutenant followed the two men down below. Lucy mustered her senses and rushed after them.

"You can't be serious," she protested. "You're not actually gonna leave him out there alone? He'll freeze to death if nothing else!"

"Quiet, ma'am! You don't know what's at stake here," cried the bearded man over his shoulder. There was a flash of fear in his eyes. "I'm doing this for all of us," he insisted through gritted teeth. His voice wavered ever so slightly as the rear carriage door loomed close.

"There must be another way. Something we can do?" pleaded Lucy, stalling for time. "We need to talk about this first – rationally!"

She slipped around the lieutenant and appeared at the bearded man's side, placing a hand on his arm as he reached the back of the train. The lieutenant intervened, wrenching Lucy's hand away.

The bearded man relinquished his ward.

"Pl– Plea–" stammered the old man, facing his captor. He spluttered again, showering his shirt and shoes with blood; a small number of flecks landed on the bearded man's boots.

"Eugh!" cried the bearded man in horror, kicking the emergency exit door wide open. Cold air rushed in. "Go!" he urged the old man, pointing to the black outside.

The whimpering geriatric shuffled half a pace towards the open doorway and turned to face his jury, imploringly.

"Go!" roared the aggressor, this time spinning the elderly martyr back around and shoving him out of the train.

The old man fell downward onto the tracks with a cry, landing heavily upon the sharp stones and timber beams. One shaky limb at a time, the splayed victim raised himself back onto all fours, a shuddering mess of weeping, coughing, and spluttering. He swayed precariously, staggering back to his feet and, blinkingly, turning to face the vessel from which he'd been ejected.

The strong, bearded assailant finished hastily mopping up every last drop of blood from both the carriage floor and his shoes. He chucked the speckled tissues out towards the old man where a gust of wind snatched them off into the darkness.

The venerable victim looked up at his executioners, clasping his trembling hands together as he shuffled back towards them. The bearded man leaned out and grabbed the emergency door, slamming it shut again. His brow was knitted, and his thick eyebrows converged downward on the bridge of his nose. The moustache covering his lip twitched as he stared out at the old man.

The lieutenant peeled away from the window, cursing. Dan took his stead, filling the vacant space next to Lucy and the bearded man.

Light spilled out from both decks, partially illuminating the wild grass and ferns swaying either side of the rails.

Lucy's attention shifted to the lieutenant's voice behind them as he spoke to the train driver via the guard's private intercom.

"A hundred yards won't be enough," interrupted the strong man, approaching the lieutenant. "Tell him we need to move at least a mile forwards if we're going to be safe."

The lieutenant revised his order to the driver. With a creaking lurch, the train began to edge forwards. Lucy turned back to the window and watched as the old man fell away into the darkness. His outstretched hand vanished, replaced by desolate stretches of track.

Something struck the right side of the carriage with a bang. Then another bang, this time from the roof, prompting screams from the top deck. The train plunged into a higher speed, throwing Lucy and Dan off balance.

The lieutenant rushed upstairs, grabbing an assault rifle as he went, closely marked by the bearded man. Dan and Lucy followed.

"Turn all the lights off!" shouted the lieutenant. "Now!"

The terrified passengers sprang into action and extinguished the reading lights. Only the dim LEDs lining the aisle remained lit.

The passengers' reflections in the windows vanished and Lucy's eyes began to adjust to the darkness outside. Glimpses of moonlit branches flickered in and out of the window view as the train continued to accelerate.

The train clattered over the tracks, loudly jostling in every direction.

"There! Out there!" cried a passenger, pointing into the darkness. As the occupants huddled to see, a second clang resonated across the roof. Lucy spun around. With a third clang the carriage ceiling buckled inwards, in the shape of a great fist. The lieutenant leapt under the metal depression and fired three rounds directly into the roof.

The passengers screamed in shock, deafened by the blast and belatedly covering their ringing ears. The carriage jolted again, sending the lieutenant off balance as the train hurtled forward at full tilt.

Lucy pressed her face to the glass and stared downward. Odd shapes flickered in and out of the lower deck's lighting spill, blending with the night. Lucy's heart skipped a beat as two dark limbs raced forwards alongside the track in great strides only to vanish as quickly as they appeared.

Two more pangs struck the carriage – this time at the rear of the top deck. With a great wrenching sound the emergency exit disappeared, ripped from its hinges entirely.

At that moment the entire world spun. Lucy was thrown into the air as the carriage revolved beneath her. The emergency lighting immediately cut out, plunging her into total darkness as the train rolled, throwing its occupants around like a blender.

Time went into slow motion as Lucy tumbled helplessly through the darkness, immersed in the screams of her fellow passengers. She ricocheted off seats, luggage racks, and bodies as the momentum flung down the carriage. In her last seconds of consciousness she registered the cold rushing air hit her face.

The story continues in

Convulsive

Part Two

Available now at
www.marcusmartin.co.uk

ABOUT THE AUTHOR

Marcus Martin began his writing career creating dramas and comedies for theatre and radio, before expanding into the world of books. He is also an avid composer and songwriter. He's currently based in Cambridge, UK, where he fell in love with the city after completing his postgraduate studies at the university.

www.marcusmartin.co.uk

Like what you

just read?

Why not support my next project?

Become a fan from just $1 per month.

Exclusive releases, updates, Q&As, and more.

Join the awesome community at:

www.patreon.com/marcusmartin

Printed in Great Britain
by Amazon